# Vintage Hearts

Susan B. Roara

Publisher's note: This is a work of fiction. Names, characters, places, and incidents either are the product of the author's imagination or are used fictitiously. Any resemblance to actual events, locales, or persons, living or dead, is entirely coincidental.

Edited, formatted, and book design by Kristen Corrects, Inc.
Cover art design by Susan B. Roara

First edition published 2017

ISBN:  10: 0-99678225-7
       13: 978-0-9967822-5-8

**TABLE OF CONTENTS**

*For my mother, Susan Mary, whose hand I often felt*
*and whose presence was always noticed.*

# CHAPTER 1

*Lucy*

It was the voice that kept her up at night, the never-ending chatter that existed in her mind. It spoke to her incessantly; it spoke to others, the disagreements and feelings that she harbored, those thoughts that she would never *dare* say out loud. The full-on arguments with Jack, the ones where she stood up for herself, the ones where she would scream, "You controlling, arrogant, judgmental son of a bitch!" She considered the look of surprise on his face when she held strong and pointed up at him, her heavy eyes angry with hurt, her voice shaking with the fear that her built-up anxiety and frustration would combust and destroy her. In her mind, she would win the fight that she replayed over and over again. He would tell her he was sorry. He would tell her that he loved her.

*That* voice.

It calmed her when she felt the anxiety, it told her everything was going to be okay, reassuring her that she could handle it, the problems she had with Jack. But the voice was complicated and strategic, manipulating thoughts that suited Lucy in moments of need. Deep down she knew that her marriage was in trouble. Even her dreams revealed those truths that were hard to ignore. The simple fact was, Lucy was failing at her life, and she felt exhausted.

She climbed into bed next to Jack, who snored deeply. She nuzzled her body under the heavy quilt and laid her head on the pillow. It wasn't long before she was startled awake in her dream, not having even realized she was asleep, by the echo of gunshots she heard outside.

She sat up in her bed. The air in the room was warm with heat. The humidity suffocated her lungs, the window glass dripped with condensation, and her hair was glued to her neckline and across her forehead. She kicked off her covers and reached for Jack but he was gone. The room was dim and glowing with an orange light that faded in and out as if a large neon sign had been placed outside her window.

The banging continued. Her body rose off the mattress, her nightgown flowing around her. She always enjoyed the weightlessness of her dreams.

She landed on her feet then tiptoed her way across the hardwood floors, her dainty toes delicate as she walked. Touching the door, she hesitated. The noise was frightening. With a shaking hand she extended her reach to the doorknob. The vintage crystal knob shined and distracted her as a ray of coral spectrum danced along her white nightgown.

The door opened.

She walked into the hallway, her feet sticking to the floor. A dark pool of blood trickled through the space like a quiet stream of water after a heavy rainstorm. The bottom of her nightgown stained red and the dark liquid oozed in between her toes. Lucy's breathing labored, as her chest rose and fell with the sound of each firing blast. She continued toward the noise. It was getting louder and pulled her forward as she followed the banging outside, away from the blood.

She paused at the edge of the porch and stared out over the horizon. The porch teetered as if on the edge of a cliff, ready to collapse at any moment. The orange glow beamed down all around her. She covered her eyes from the brightness and glanced over the side. The gunshots continued, ringing in her ears and tempting her to duck out of harm's way, but there was only empty vastness all around her. Her heart was racing, the blood was pouring through her house and out of the windows.

It was coming for her. She needed to jump.

The voice was talking, convincing her that this was the only way out. She felt alone. Images of her small children appeared as they called for her, "MOM! MOM! MOM!" She closed her eyes, a flash of parental doubt flooding her body. Her arms raised, she willed herself to hang on, to do better.

But it was coming.

She leaned over the edge of the cliff and let go. She let go of her reservation, her devotion. The wind stripped her fears away from her soul and her spirit soared freely through the air.

She fell, the noise behind her, the blood flowing over the cliff like a waterfall. She squeezed her eyes and screamed for her life. She screamed for her freedom.

She held her breath, and he caught her. Standing at the bottom, with his arms held tight, he reached for her and she landed in his arms. He placed her on her feet.

*Nicholas.*

Lucy sprung up from her pillow, her body damp with moisture. She jumped out of bed and ran into the bathroom, leaned over the sink and splashed water onto her face.

She hadn't thought about him in years.

Something awful was about to happen. She shook her head, and made the sign of the cross. She prayed her dreams weren't premonitions. Nick was coming for her and something bad was about to happen. Maybe she was wrong, but as an intuitive, she was rarely ever wrong.

Lucy returned to her bed. She lay as close to Jack as she could, taking his arms and wrapping them around her until she could barely breathe.

She was safe in his arms—Jack's arms.

But Nicholas was coming for her.

# CHAPTER 2

## *Nicholas*

He bounded down the stairs to the basement in three long jumps, landing roughly at the bottom. His safe had been pried open. His loaded bookshelf had been tipped over and pushed to the floor, scattering his collection of old detective novels and police procedural manuals. He stepped over the file cabinet that hung dangerously between the floor and the chair that stopped its impending fall. Bending down, he inspected the safe, which was empty. His antique Colt firearm was gone, along with the cash and the watch, his *father's* watch. He slammed the safe door shut, smashing his fist against the wall. "FUCK!"

Nicholas moved toward his desk and sat down, leaning back in his chair. He stared at the large clock in the corner of his office. The ticking silence of the small, simple room seemed to hypnotize him. He was thinking rapidly but his thoughts were riddled with anger and frustration. The heaviness in his shoulders felt familiar as pains of stress pinched his neck muscles.

11

Leaning forward, he began checking his gun safety and bullet supply. He looked at his hand, turning it over and over. Blood trickled from his knuckles and he was still shaking. He tried to steady his temper, taking deep, cleansing breaths, but it wasn't working. He flung a pile of paperwork off his desk to scatter through the air and across the floor. His mind was confused and he struggled to collect his thoughts, trying to focus and proceed with a plan, but he felt helplessly incompetent.

He gathered himself, picked up his phone then dialed his partner. "Alex, I need your help," he said. Nicholas held the phone out in front of him, his eyes glazed over, feeling disconnected from the phone and the person on the other end. Nicholas could hardly recognize his own voice. He had never felt this way, weak and vulnerable. He was an excellent detective, a man who had solved many cases, a man with conviction and strength. He was a man who told *others* what to do. This feeling, what he felt now, was foreign. He struggled to understand it.

This was his family. This was a whole knew ballgame.

Nicholas could hear Alex pause on the other end of the phone, then his voice came through clearly. "I'll be right there, Nick. Don't do anything foolish, I'll be right over."

Nick hung up the phone.

He peeled himself away from the desk and moved throughout his house. The lovely furniture his wife spent months selecting for their home was overturned, glass windows shattered and broken, electronics stolen. Nicholas thought about his young family, safe on vacation in Martha's Vineyard. He thought about his wife Beth, how angry she had been that he was unable to join them on their holiday. Nick's obsession and commitment to his career was once again interfering with their family time, and Beth was very vocal about her dissatisfaction.

Beth's fears that Nick's profession would someday jeopardize her and her children's safety had always been unjustified, but as Nick scanned over his ruined home, he realized they were now a reality. He knew who was responsible for the break-in. He knew the threats were to be taken seriously and that his wife was right—they were in danger. He thought he could protect them, that they would be safe under his watch, but he was wrong and reckless to think that he could control that scumbag son of a bitch, Anthony Massimo.

Nick ascended the stairs toward the bedrooms. He entered his youngest daughter's room, seeing her bed and mattress overturned, her clothes scattered about. His eyes narrowed in on the wall, once decorated with rainbows and fairies, now scrawled with a message.

Nicholas felt his face drop and his eyes swell as he looked up at the graffiti, a message meant only for him. "How does it feel?" he spoke out loud. "It feels fucking awful," he screamed, picked up a toy and threw it across the room, smashing his daughter's dresser mirror. He sat on her bed and was overwhelmed by the emotions sucking at his strength and reserve. Tears fell from his face as angry, guttural noises escaped from a place deep down within him.

He allowed himself the moment to suffer and anguish over dreadful thoughts. What could have happened? What if they were home, his family, his beautiful children, and their round and innocent faces, their bright eyes and tiny frames? The feelings and thoughts were so overpowering that he ignored the phone beside him on the bed as it rang, vibrating across the coverlet. He closed his eyes and tried to catch his breath, feeling fear and panic as he struggled to wrap his mind around what he was going to do next. Police sirens echoed in the far distance. Help was on the way, yet he remained unmoved. He could hear pounding on his front door and the voices of the police officers as they entered his house.

"Nick! Nick!"

Alex screamed his name as he and three other detectives bounded up the stairs, their guns drawn. Nicholas wiped the reverie

14

from his face and glanced up into the doorway where his lifelong friend and partner stood. Nick focused on Alex. The understanding between the two men was deep and impenetrable.

"Anthony Massimo, he did this," Nicholas ground out. "He was just released from prison. I know he's responsible." He closed his eyes and said the words that Alex had been waiting to hear, for *five long* years now.

"We are going to Mexico."

# CHAPTER 3

*Anthony*

The walls were cinderblock; a pewter grey tone that over time began to look yellowed and faded. The paint job was peeling and the shelf that hung midway up the wall was layered with dust and small particles that fell from the ceiling above. The room was small and simple: a cot for a bed, a small desk and toilet. It was the last room at the end of a long hallway, twenty cells before it. The bars were a metallic grey, offering some view of the outside hall.

Anthony Massimo had spent five years in this room and he had never gotten used to the confining space. He stared obsessively at the pictures of his family taped to the wall, touching them frequently and kissing them often. He spoke to himself, mumbling words angrily: "Like a caged animal, I'm kept." Other days he would repeat more positive words, the prayers his mother taught him when he was young: "Our father, who art in Heaven…"

Anthony sat on his cot and stared, remembering the overwhelming depression, the isolation, and the deprivation of his life's daily pleasures. He fought back for years, struggling to keep his mind active, relentless in keeping his body in shape as he waited to mark the end of his prison term. He vowed to live his life with passion and appreciation for whatever may come his way. It was a promise to the Lord that he made over and over again that he would do better, if only he could be granted a second chance.

The cell doors opened. Two guards stood awaiting him, and he turned so they could secure his wrists behind him. The handcuffs were tight.

Anthony walked out of his holding cell for the last time. He looked back at the encompassing room and spat into the empty space, soon to be filled by another drug dealing criminal. He walked down the constitutional halls of the prison with the armed guards, voices of his fellow inmates filling the air.

"Good luck Anthony! Don't forget about us," said one prisoner.

"You'll be back here soon enough, you son of a bitch."

"Have a drink for me, man," said another.

Anthony smiled at his alleged friends, knowing deep down inside that he would never see them again. His smile couldn't convey the deep satisfaction he felt, now that he was somehow better than them. He was going to be on the outside looking in.

The security guards escorted him past the inner sanction of the prison. He thought about the friends he had made over the past five years. He thought about his business associates and the dirt bags he'd grown accustomed to throughout his entire life. They meant nothing to him now. They were beneath him in many ways but mostly, Anthony felt smarter than them.

Anthony had never been a reader, but he hoarded stacks of books from the prison library. Some of them he read for pleasure, others he read because he wanted to feel intelligent. Reading had saved him; the stories had opened his mind and broadened his intellect.

He thought about his family. He thought about his beautiful wife Rose, who was still married to him. Her continued support often surprised Anthony, as he knew that he was not worthy of her attention, let alone her uncompromised commitment to him. On their wedding day she had vowed she would never leave him, and she kept her promise. She stood by him, thick and thin. He found her miraculous, as special to him as a child would be to his mother. Her loyalty was unmoving and awe inspiring; she was a decent person. Anthony was not.

His thoughts wandered to his son, who had grown without him, five years of childhood memories gone. Anthony marveled at how respectful and smart Jase was, prideful at the fact that Rose and Jase continued to be a strong family, even in the face of his incarceration. He was grateful for his wife, her strength and integrity making all the difference in his son's life.

He would soon be with them, moments away from seeing them and breathing the fresh clean air of freedom. His heart beat faster.

His exit interview and meeting with the probation officials went well as he portrayed the feeling that he was "rehabilitated." In fact, he never felt rehabilitated; he knew his life was beyond repair. But he answered the questions, he knew all the right responses and he was respectful. One thing Anthony had learned in prison was that respect meant different things to different people. When he was young, he thought that it was fool arrogance and violence that demanded respect from his fellow associates. Now he understood what respect meant. It meant that you were smart. He couldn't earn people's respect if he continued to be a fool—and he was going to be nobody's fool.

Anthony walked through the final doors of the prison's internal structure and squinted as he was suddenly outside in the secured parking lot. He could see his wife's car, his son bouncing around in the backseat. Rose opened the door, stepping out of the vehicle. Her smile was reassuring, her beauty stunning as she opened the back door for her son.

Jase exited the vehicle and ran toward his father. Anthony dropped his meager possessions, scooped his young son into his arms, and swung him around while holding him tight.

"Papa, Papa...you can come home now!" Jase held his father's cheeks with his small hands. "I missed you so much, Papa."

Anthony held his five-year-old son in his arms and squeezed him to his chest. "I missed you, buddy. Everything will be alright now."

Anthony reached for his wife and pulled her into him. He kissed her softly.

"Are you ready to go home, Anthony?" she asked. "Your family is waiting for you."

Anthony smiled as his wife threw him the keys to their vehicle. He turned back to look at the fortress of the prison. The fifteen-foot fence topped by barbed wire dared any prisoner to climb its height to get to the other side of freedom. Beyond that, acres of green fields surrounded them, and the barren feeling that there was nothing else out there. These were all going to be distant memories for him, moments he would block forever.

He thanked the Lord for this opportunity to be whole again, to be a part of his family.

He started the vehicle, relishing the feel of the power under his feet, and wondered if he still had a valid license in his wallet. It didn't matter. It felt good to drive, he felt like a man again.

He was free.

And he was smart now. He wasn't going to screw this up.

# CHAPTER 4

## *Charles*

Charles ambled down the street in the direction of his apartment building. He walked along the asphalt curb, which crumbled away from the sidewalk, and on occasion, he moved into the street to avoid making contact with the random garbage can. Urgency pushed him forward. His eyes focused straight ahead as he tucked his hands nervously into his pants pocket. Beads of sweat layered his upper lip, and his face paled. He entered a side alleyway and vomited. He let the dry heaves wrack his body as he steadied himself against the brick of the building.

He hated this. He hated feeling sick more than anything. He tried—every day he tried to go without the pills and every day he became sick. It was becoming routine, to vomit, his body rejecting anything good and healthy. "Fuck!" he spat as he shook his head.

The voice inside him told him that he was turning into one of those guys, like the crack heads that begged him for work every morning at the corner. They would stand around, asking for money, promising a good day's effort in exchange. Charles knew what they were. They were useless, pieces of shit drug addicts who couldn't wake up straight. He knew not to give them any of his hard-earned money. He wasn't one of them—he was different. It wasn't his fault, the way he was. He had it all under control.

He straightened up. He continued down the sidewalk again, nauseous still, and he managed to make it to his apartment. He walked through the front door and dropped his heavy fishing boots onto the mat in the hallway. Kat sat at the table waiting for him.

"Hey," she said dryly.

"Hey," he replied as he moved through the kitchen.

Kat never smiled at him anymore. Charles supposed she didn't have much to smile about.

"We need to talk, Charles," she continued as he brushed past her. Every day was the same. Every day he came home to her and every day, she wanted to talk.

"I'm tired, Kat," he replied as he entered the bathroom, closing the door behind him. He opened the medicine cabinet, pulled out a bottle of pills, and shook it. One pill danced in the otherwise empty container. He opened it, shoved the pill in his mouth, and closed his eyes. He would never make it through the evening with only one pill. He would suffer...and it was his birthday today. It didn't seem fair to him that he should suffer on his birthday.

He opened his cell phone.

"Can you meet me in thirty minutes?" he murmured to the stranger. "Yeah, I have the money, I'll get you what I owe you, just bring the pills." Charles hung up the phone.

A scattered pile of bills and paperwork layered the dining room table, many of which seemed to glow with bright red lettering, *Second Notice* written across the fronts. Some bills Kat didn't even bother to look at; they just made their way into the garbage can next to her. Charles watched her as she ran her hands through her tangled hair and began to massage her temples.

"I'm getting a headache," she mumbled, not bothering to look up to see if Charles was even listening.

They were being evicted from their apartment.

Kat sat back and reached for the marijuana joint in the ashtray. She lit it and took a drag. Charles watched her close her eyes as she held the intoxicating smoke for as long as she could before she exhaled, watching the smoke fill the air in the space from which she breathed.

She picked up an invitation sitting on top of the bills and held it up to show Charles. "It's from Lucy. It's for Pop's eightieth birthday party. They want us to come. It would be a long trip but maybe it would be good for us," Kat said. She stared at him and waited. Charles remained silent. "Charles?"

Charles glanced up. He had been staring at his untied shoelace. He bent over and started to tie it.

"Where are you going now?" she asked, her voice grating.

"I need to go out for a bit, why?"

"Did you hear me, about the party?"

"Yeah, I'll think about it."

She sighed. "We need money, Charles. Did you catch any fish today? We can't keep ignoring our landlord. He sent us another eviction notice."

Charles inhaled a deep breath. He had a few extra hundred dollars he could probably give her, but he would rather wait until tomorrow. Maybe he'd make a big catch and then he wouldn't have to worry about the money.

"Tomorrow's catch will be better, Kat. We *will* catch up, I promise you."

She scoffed. "You can't keep saying that, Charles. Look at the bills we have piled up here." Kat reached for a stack and fanned it in Charles' face. He threw his head back to avoid being hit by it.

"What the fuck, Kat?"

"Oh I'm sorry," she said sarcastically. "Perhaps if I hit you with them, maybe you wouldn't ignore them so easily."

Charles felt his face growing red. He was beginning to sweat again, he wasn't feeling well, and Kat and the bills were the last things on his mind.

"You look like shit, by the way. I'm starting to worry about you. I think you need to be around your family," Kat said. "Maybe your brother could help you." She made her way to Charles and wrapped her arms around his body. "I just want us to be happy, Charles. Happy birthday, by the way."

Charles glared down into her face, trying to conjure some sort of feelings for her. It had been a rough few years between them. Her lack of employment was stressful on their relationship and he in general was beginning to dislike her. He leaned in and spoke clearly in Kat's face. "Why don't you get up off your lazy ass and get a job for once? Maybe that would be more helpful, Kat."

Kat recoiled, retreating across the kitchen. "You're an asshole. You know I've been trying to find a job."

"Yeah well, sitting around all day smoking pot isn't a solution, Kat."

"I'm not the only one here with a problem, Charles," she said, her voice equally tinged with malice. "Let's not forget."

Charles grabbed his coat and walked toward the front door.

Kat reached out for him and grabbed his arm. "No wait! Please Charles, don't go, we still need to talk. Don't leave me yet, we can figure this out."

Charles pushed her away from him and opened the door to leave. He looked back at her and watched her as she began to cry. "Crying isn't going to help, Kat. Finding some money would." He slammed the door shut behind him.

He paused in the hallway to see if she would follow. She didn't. He was beginning to feel the effects from the pill; relief flooded his body. He didn't think about Kat. He thought about the pills. That's all he ever thought about.

The pills made it better for him.

# CHAPTER 5

*Nicholas*

Nick moved the curtain away from the front living room window, watching for any unfamiliar vehicles as he waited for Beth to return from vacation. Piles of white and stained drop clothes along with large boxes of new TVs and stereo equipment crowded the front door, making the entire hallway almost unmanageable. He sighed. Beth had abruptly hung up on him earlier after he tried to prepare her for the messy house. He knew he would have to explain to her why he was renovating their home, but he dreaded her hateful stare, her condescending smirk, and the "I told you so" attitude.

She had packed her bags in the past, abandoning him to go live with her mother in Long Island. Her childhood home came equipped with a large swimming pool, maid service, and round-the-clock nanny care. Beth never tired of reminding Nicholas how she sacrificed for him, marrying down financially and how his job was a danger to her and her children. Nicholas often argued, "You knew what you were getting into when you married me!" But all of that didn't matter now. Her fears had turned into a reality as Nick looked around his home, remembering what it had looked like only a few days before, with broken glass everywhere, missing appliances, and ruined furniture.

Nicholas thought about Lucy.

He had never asked her for her assistance before, although he had thought about it many times. She had a special gift; her ability to receive signs and interpret dreams could be valuable in his search for the men who had threatened his family.

Kat and Charles still worked out of Boston harbor close to the police station, which made it easy for Nick to occasionally bump into them. Kat was always happy to see him; her big embrace and proud smile reassured him that what he did for a living was important. The people he worked with and helped obviously cared for him, as he did for them. Even Charles seemed to grow fond of Nicholas over time, eager to visit and to share a beer. They were all on good terms, but Nicholas' motivation to see them was always Lucy. He needed to know that she was okay.

He remembered the little things about her. She was so vulnerable to him, the way her round, blue eyes pled with him, begging him to help her. She thanked him time and time again for saving her sister's life. He smiled to himself, remembering how sweet and innocent she was back then and how confused she was over her intuitive talent.

Nick walked over to the phone and picked up the receiver. He pulled out Lucy's phone number, which he had kept in his wallet for years now. He paused and looked at it. He wanted to call her so many times. His hands were sweaty against the back of the receiver; he wasn't sure how to approach the phone call. Perhaps he could have tried harder with Lucy years ago; perhaps he should never have left her with Jack.

It was complicated.

He wondered though, if things had been different, had they met more casually and without all the drama, would they have had a chance?

Nicholas considered his own marriage and reluctantly accepted that Lucy had probably made the right choice; Nicholas and Lucy's life together would have been strained, just as it was now with his current wife.

This didn't stop him, however, from knowing what Lucy was doing with herself. How many children did she have, where did she live? He knew everything about her, yet he knew nothing about her, holding on to a memory that seemed more like a fantasy than anything else. Their relationship had once been built upon a blind trust and respect. Lucy needed him during a frantic moment in her

30

life, and he desperately needed to be needed. Either way, Nicholas had always kept a safe and unobtrusive distance from her. But he loved her, unexplainably. He loved her.

He could use her help now. He wondered if she would be willing.

Nicholas heard his wife's car pull up the driveway and put the receiver back down in its place. He walked toward the front door to open it, greeting his wife and children with a warm and loving smile.

Beth exited the car and pushed past him, holding on to their youngest son as she rushed through the front door.

"Hello Beth," Nicholas said as she continued into the house.

"Go fuck yourself," she spat. Nicholas cringed from her tone; the lack of grace and restraint around their children was irritating. He closed his eyes briefly, then took a deep breath. When he opened them, his four-year-old daughter was standing at his feet, her arms held up toward his, eager for him to lift her up gently and into an embrace.

"Hello Daddy," she said sweetly. Nick smiled down at his daughter and held her tight in his arms.

"Hello baby," he said.

"I missed you, Daddy."

"I missed you too, sweetheart."

Nick held on to his daughter for a few minutes, relishing their time together. Just as swiftly as he felt her joy, he suddenly felt that parental fear strike him in his stomach. Thoughts of what could have happened to his daughter dominated his mind as unprovoked visions of her innocent helplessness made his heart ache with pain.

He would call Lucy. He needed to do everything in his power to end this fight with Anthony Massimo and to keep his family safe. He needed to do it for his children. All common sense and rationalizations were off the table as Nick made his final decision.

Lucy needed to help him; she needed to go to Mexico with him, he decided. She owed him this one last favor.

# CHAPTER 6

## *Charles*

Charles stuffed money in a sock and shoved it underneath a pile of clothes in his suitcase. A few days earlier he stood in line at the pawnshop and gave the man behind the counter an antique watch along with several old coins that he had stolen. The cautious pawnshop owner had eyed Charles, but Charles didn't worry. Charles was careful when he pawned robbed items. He stored his inventory in an unused old janitor's closet in the basement of his apartment building. He took his time offing the electronics, the jewelry, and the antiques to avoid suspicion.

He and Kat arrived in Indiana for Pop's birthday a day early after having their reservations about going. Charles unpacked his bag, throwing on top of his clothes the bottles of his pain medication that he had stockpiled just for the occasion.

It wasn't comfortable, being on the farm with his family. His face hurt from pretending, conversing with Jack and Pop as if he felt normal and had a normal life. The apple orchards just beyond Pop's farmhouse, a quarter mile walk of nature and pleasantry, offered Charles the only sanctuary he could find. He stood on top of the orchard's hill and overlooked the farm, thinking. Why hadn't his life been so plush? How did he miss out on all this, his grandfather having so much to offer him?

Charles could see Pop waiting for him in the driveway as he made his way from the orchard to the house. He met him halfway and Pop placed his arm around his shoulder. "You made it, boy. I feel honored you took the trip all this way to see me. It means a lot, Charles. You're a good man."

"Yeah, no problem, Pop," Charles ground out. "I'm happy to be back. Looks like you and Jack have been busy. The farm looks great. I was just walking around, taking it all in. The new winery is impressive."

"That's all Jack and Lucy. The weekend wine tastings and the grape harvest from the past few years have been very successful. You should be very proud of your brother; he works hard."

Charles looked at his grandfather. He wanted to be proud of Jack. Jack did the smart things; he leached on to his grandfather early on in life. He had a good upbringing, with love and a family.

Pop looked away from him and Charles rolled his eyes. He didn't know Pop all that well. They were family, but strangers still.

"Anyway, what about you, Charles? How's the commercial fishing going? You and Kat making it along okay?"

Charles glanced up at his grandfather, aware of his sudden opportunity, his eyes swiftly open and engaged. "Pop, we are having some financial problems. My boat needs some engine work; it's going to be costly. I could use a little help…but I'm sure I could figure it out." Charles lowered his eyes.

"How much do you need, Charles?"

"It's going to cost at least ten thousand dollars."

Pop started to choke, then laughed. "Ten thousand dollars?!"

Charles' face dropped dramatically. This wasn't a joke to him. This was his livelihood. "Forget I mentioned it, Pop."

Pop cleared his throat while Charles stood in silence. "Ten thousand dollars, huh?" Pop thought a moment. "Well, I've got some work here on the farm that needs to be done. I need a new roof on the barn; we have another orchard to plant. Maybe if you stick around for a few weeks, we could work something out, you and I. I would pay you for your time."

"A few weeks?" Charles murmured. He didn't have enough pills for a few weeks. "I appreciate the offer Pop, but—"

35

"Well, think about it, Charles. You don't have to answer me right now. I'd like to help out if I can."

Pop slapped Charles on his shoulder and walked off down the driveway toward the barn. The old man probably had a boatload of money, yet he was going to make Charles work for it.

Jack's truck pulled into the driveway as Charles walked over to it, still annoyed with Pop and their conversation. He slammed the door shut, the glass window rattling within its metal frame.

"What's your problem?" Jack asked.

Charles put on a smile, realizing he must be glowering. "Nothing," he replied under his breath.

"Are we doing this or what?" Jack asked.

Jack needed Charles' help to move a small herd of cattle away from the vineyard and back into the upper fields.

"Yeah, screw it. I'll do what I can."

Jack smiled mischievously. "We need to get on some horses."

Charles shrugged his shoulders. He needed money, and a damn good reason to stay on the farm. "Well, it looks like I've got nothing to lose," Charles conceded.

Jack laughed out loud.

"That's an understatement, Charles!"

# CHAPTER 7

*Lucy*

Lucy walked through the French doors of the wine tasting room. She scanned the space thoroughly, hoping she didn't miss a detail. The old farm tables were glowing with candles and decorated with tall vases of bright purple lilac. The rafters and the arched entranceways sparkled with holiday lights.

The winery orchards' first vines were planted three years ago, and the bar was stocked now with their finest vintage wine. It was Pop's birthday and the room was crowded with friends and family. Lucy wandered through the outdoor patios.

"Hello!" She waved as she greeted as many guests as she could, strolling along the brick walkways and overlooking the view of the orchards, glowing in the setting sun's light.

She scanned the open area for Jack. She caught his eye and walked toward him. The black strapless cocktail dress she wore fit her like a glove and she moved effortlessly, catching the stares of her guests as she walked past them.

Jack smiled and moved away from the bar and took her hand. His eyes were soft.

She searched his face. "Jack?"

"You look lovely," he murmured. He wrapped his arm around her lower back and guided her through the party.

"Good evening, Mr. Jenkins," Lucy said as she kissed her elderly neighbor on his cheek.

"Hello dear," he responded. She smiled easily. She glanced around to see if the caterers had started to serve the hors d'oeuvres. She hoped the bartenders were sharing their most recent wines and pouring their guest glasses generously. She glanced frequently at Jack, hoping she didn't forget anything, hoping he was pleased with her.

"Lucy!" Pop hollered through the crowd. Lucy waved and indicated that she'd be right over.

Jack bent down and whispered in her ear, "Did you set out Pop's gift? The eighty-year-old Cabernet that I had ordered, specifically for his birthday?"

Lucy's eyes widened. "It's in the wine cellar. I'll say hello and run downstairs to get it." Oh god, the wine. Jack went out of his way to find this special wine, harvested in a small town in Italy, the town where Pop's family came from.

Jack frowned and turned his back on her, addressing other partygoers.

Lucy rolled her eyes. She could feel her shoulders slouch slightly. She knew she would forget something but continued to move across the room as Pop beckoned her to come to him.

"Hey Pop," she said as she hugged him.

"Why the face?" he asked as he held her tight.

"Oh, it's nothing. Happy birthday!" she said.

"Thank you Lucy, the party is absolutely beautiful. Susie Mae and I are so proud of you; it's been a very special night.

"Thank you Pop. Have you eaten anything? Have they started to serve the food?"

"Yes. The food, Lucy, it's delicious! What about you? Stop and eat before you get too busy socializing."

"Yeah, I will, I promise. I need to do a few things first, but enjoy the party, Pop."

Lucy reached over and kissed him on his cheek. "Have fun, I'll be back shortly." She turned to leave.

She pushed her way through the crowd, stopping to say hello to Kat who had been laughing and enjoying the good taste of wine. "Have you seen Charles?" Kat yelled. Lucy looked around the noisy crowd and let out a deep breath and smiled. Everyone was having fun.

"I haven't, but if I do, I'll tell him you're looking for him."

"It's not important," Kat mentioned. "Where are you going anyway?" she asked as Lucy walked away.

"I need to grab something downstairs!"

"Wait a minute, take a glass of wine at least. You of all people need a drink!"

Lucy took the offered wine and smirked at her sister. Kat was right—she needed to relax a bit and enjoy herself. Stop stressing about everything.

She finally made it to the back of the barn and took the flight of stairs down to the wine cellar. She was always impressed when she walked through its glass doors. The room was large with high ceilings. Jack had cleared an acre of trees from their first orchard of vines. He milled every beam, every plank board, and all of the shelving and material. That was three years ago; now they had

41

ten acres of vines and two large barrel-aging rooms and a full wine cellar. It was very impressive.

She walked along, careful not to trip on the fieldstone flooring. She placed her hand along the row of her oldest vintage bottles, trying to remember where she placed Pop's wine. She tapped each bottle with her fingertip, listening to the clicking sound of her newly manicured fingernails.

"It's quite a stash you and Jack have," Charles spoke from behind her. Lucy whipped her head around; her hand covered her chest as she laughed nervously.

"Charles! You scared me!" Lucy eyed him. "What are you doing down here? I didn't see you when I came in." Charles walked around her, staggering. He reached for a wine bottle and placed it on the counter.

"I think you're looking for this," he said. Lucy scanned the bottle's label and realized it was exactly what she was looking for.

"Jack shouldn't send you downstairs, alone in the basement."

"Yeah, well, I wasn't exactly expecting anyone here. Perhaps you should go upstairs now, and join the party. Kat's been looking for you."

Charles nodded his head but remained unmoving. He poured himself another glass of wine, emptying his bottle. He raised his glass to Lucy.

"To you and Jack!" he stated. "You've been blessed." Charles drank the entire glass in one gulp.

"Yes. Okay well, thank you, Charles. I'll see you upstairs." Lucy climbed the staircase and searched for Jack, handing him the bottle of wine, and then pulling him aside.

"I need to talk to you."

"Not now, Lucy."

"It's important, please.

"Excuse me Paul, I just need a minute."

Lucy dragged Jack toward the kitchen area behind the bar.

"Jack, I went into the basement, like you asked, and Charles was there. He scared the hell out of me. He was there drinking, and he was acting very strange. Something's not right with your brother."

Jack looked exasperated. "What are you talking about, Lucy?"

"I don't know Jack, but he gives me the creeps."

Jack rolled his eyes. "Really, Lucy? Tonight's the night you're going to start in on my family?

Lucy's heart sunk. She didn't want to start anything.

"Jack," she implored as she reached out to touch his arm.

"Forget it, Lucy." His voice was bitter. "I'm going back to the party."

Lucy followed him. They entered the party and she saw Charles standing across the room with Kat. Jack raised his glass to him, Charles responded. Jack glanced down at Lucy.

His glare was familiar. She sank back out of the building and off onto the patio, where Jack wasn't, where it was quiet and peaceful. She sat alone on a stone bench, overlooking the orchard and listening to the quiet chatter of her guests as they held private conversations all around her. She had done everything she could, everything she could think of to make tonight perfect, and she still felt like he disapproved of her. She lowered her eyes and stared at her wedding ring, turning it around and around on her finger. She sighed.

Lucy glanced up into the large full-length glass windows of the winery building. She could see Kat making her way through the crowd and outside, straight for her.

"Come with me quick, I need help with Charles."

Lucy put her drink down and walked with Kat, around to the front of the building. Charles was there, swaying as his feet moved around nervously. He staggered toward them.

"What's his problem?" Lucy whispered to Kat.

"He gets like this sometimes, really drunk. He just needs to go to bed," Kat explained.

Lucy knew that this was more than sometimes, that perhaps Charles had a major problem with alcohol.

"Okay Charles, Lucy and I are going to take you home," Kat stated calmly.

Charles focused on them and he chuckled to himself. "Two dumb bitches," he muttered.

"What's that?" Lucy asked. Her eyes narrowed in on her brother-in-law, ashamed to call him family. "Hold on Kat, let me go get Jack for help. This seems a bit more than we can handle."

Charles turned on Lucy and stopped her before she entered the building. "I don't need help, little girl. I'll make it home *just* fine," he sneered at her.

Lucy ripped her arm away from Charles, standing back and staring at him, the wine beginning to sour in her stomach. "Please Charles, leave now before you upset anyone. This is supposed to be a special night for Pop. Go now, go back to the house and rest." Lucy encouraged Charles down the driveway and away from the party. Perhaps it was for the best Jack didn't know about this; he would probably blame her for it anyway.

Charles stumbled away on his own, away from Lucy and Kat. "Well, I wouldn't want to mess with your precious party," he stated, tripping and catching himself before falling.

Kat waved. "Bye-bye, Charles. I'll see you later."

Charles whistled, an eerie reminder filling the air as he disappeared around the corner.

"Well, that was fun," Kat stated as she walked back into the building.

Lucy raised her eyes toward her sister, not sure if she should get into it with her. She decided not to; it would only cause more problems.

Lucy entered the party, just in time to hear Pop's speech.

"…and to Jack."

Pop held out his wineglass to Jack. "This old man and this farm, I couldn't do it without you. You fill me with pride. Every day I am amazed at what you can accomplish and I'm proud to call you my son. I love you, Jack."

Lucy smiled as she watched her husband hug his grandfather.

"And Lucy, my sweet girl," Pop continued, seeing her on the edge of the crowd, "you are a gift to us all, the one who ensures that I will have warm wool socks all winter long." The crowd laughed. "Your attention to each of us is heartwarming, we love you like our own, and I wish you both great success and a lifetime of happiness. Thank you for this wonderful party. I will never forget it."

Lucy made her way to Pop and wrapped her arms around him, hugging him tight.

He always made her feel special, even though it was *he* who kept them all together. "Thank you Pop," she murmured.

"I love you."

# CHAPTER 8

*Lucy*

Jack's breaths came in and out as he slept beside Lucy. Her eyes fluttered back and forth, but she refused to open them. She was awake. It was too early to be awake, she knew, but she felt uneasy. Worry had started to circle around her thoughts. She removed Jack's arm from around her chest, rose from the bed, and struggled to find some of her clothing that had been carelessly thrown aside the night before. The party was over.

The headache was eminent as she remembered Jack, filling her last glass of wine. She tiptoed out of her bedroom and past her children's rooms without alerting anyone. She needed coffee, a strong cup of coffee in a quiet, sleeping household.

Her thoughts were heavy as she tried to recall all the moments and conversations from the night before. Her stomach rumbled within her, causing her to feel off balanced. She searched in her cupboard for aspirin and looked for an appealing snack. Her stomach turned again and a flow of heat ran throughout her body as she stabled herself against the kitchen table. Her hands shook as she poured herself the steaming black liquid. She stared out the dining room window and watched as the sun made its appearance over the orchards. Even the chickens were still and quiet, nesting noiselessly in their hen house. She looked down at Pop's farm and at the remnants of the party. The white tent flaps moved in the early morning breeze, and debris and scattered garbage littered the grounds along with the occasional toppled chair. The property was deserted, void of all life except for the occasional scavenging animal scrapping for food. They would have a lot of cleanup today, more than her alcohol-battered body could endure, possibly. Although she enjoyed the occasional glass of wine, she didn't drink often and now she remembered why.

Lucy swallowed her first sip of coffee and felt the hot liquid flow past her lips and burn down the back of her throat. The bitter coffee was unforgiving against her nervous stomach. She tried to move around, hoping to shake off the unexplainable feeling of panic. She closed her eyes and listened to her quiet, peaceful house. Her chest rose and fell rapidly and she wondered if she were going to get sick. The palms of her hands were sweaty with perspiration; her hair stuck to the back of her neck.

St. Peter's Church bell began to ring, the call of early morning filling the quiet space between their farm and town. She walked toward the front of her little farmhouse and opened the door. The fresh crisp breeze was welcoming and calmed and cooled her body. Her toes touched the damp front porch. The sound of sirens filled the air. She could see a police cruiser speeding past their farm. An ambulance appeared behind it, giving chase. Lucy watched as they past their farm and went straight for Pop's. Although she was frozen, her thoughts went wild with confusion and assumptions, mindful explanations trying to convince herself that everything was fine. Her body's physical rejection screamed differently.

The phone rang. She ran toward it, answering it breathlessly, "Hello?"

"Lucy, it's Pop. He's been hurt. You need to come," Kat said urgently. Lucy stood motionless, listening as her coffee mug slipped from her hand, watching the glass shatter across the checkered kitchen floor.

"*Jack!*" she screamed, her voice trembling as within her rose that long-ago forgotten feeling of dread.

# CHAPTER 9

## *Anthony*

Anthony settled into his family's home in the small town of Chapala, Mexico. It was an easy decision to be made, yet it was difficult on so many other levels. The one thing Anthony feared the most about moving back to Mexico was living in close proximity to the centralized crime and drug exportation out of Guadalajara. Anthony's old employer, Mr. Garcia, still owned and operated Global Exportation, one of Mexico's fastest-growing trade companies. A seemingly legal outfit, Global Exportation was riddled with corruption and illegal activity.

Deciding to keep a low profile, staying away from socializing in the local taverns and reaching out to old friends was necessary for Anthony. Old associates were no good for him now; they held no place in his life.

He sat at the kitchen table writing in his daily journal, mesmerized by the silence. He thought about his wife. "Rose." He

51

stated her name in a hushed whisper, his tone deep and meaningful. He ran his fingers over the tattoo on his forearm, the innocent portrait of the thorn-riddled flower weaving around the inside of his wrist like a vine winding up a trellis. Rose was the most extraordinary woman he had ever known. Her name was as graceful and elegant as her curved silhouette. Much like the delicate flower, she was deceiving. Her spirit was strong and sharp, more so like the thorns that riddled the bushes that produced the beautiful blossoms. Her lips were the brightest of reds, her eyes fierce and dark, and her face round and disarmingly beautiful.

She was a strong and attractive woman, passionate for those she loved and fearless to protect her family. Much like the thorns, she could draw blood at any moment, if threatened and if she so desired. How he got so lucky to have her, he would never understand. But she supported him wholeheartedly and without question.

Anthony thought back to when he first met his wife at a little local tavern, just blocks from where they lived now.

They sat at the bar and talked for hours. They faced each other with interest, their knees touching one another, Anthony's hand resting casually on Rose's tan and shapely thighs. She begged him to dance, grabbing hold of his arms and pulling him close to her, dragging him toward the deserted dance floor. She made him look elegant and graceful as she guided him through the salsa, the music spirited, her energy lively. Anthony obliged her wishes, but soon enveloped Rose into his arms, overwhelmed with the need to feel her body pressed up against his, and he slowed their dance to a subtle rock. His chest pounded as he allowed his hands to slide down the small of her back, his face bent into the softest parts of her neck, her skin delicate and scented, her face calm and relaxed as she relented to his gentle touch with anticipation.

"Rose," he whispered, "I may never be the same again." He lifted her chin, his eyes penetrating hers deeply, pausing before his lips met hers in a soft and breathless kiss. She grabbed his hand and pulled him into the back hallway, away from the bar and away from the music.

"*Te necesito*," she whispered. Her voice was heavy with aggression as she placed her hands underneath his shirt, the sleeve of her dress falling off her shoulder. Anthony ran his fingers across her soft and heaving breast line. He glanced down the hallway, aware that they could get caught, but then pulled her to him, lifting her dress; he filled his hands with the roundness of her bottom and kissed her. Rose moaned deeply, and unbuttoning his pants, she slid her hand in between his legs. Anthony boosted her with ease as she wrapped her legs around his waist. He lowered her onto him and watched her face as she threw her head back, her exposed breast begging for his attention. He pressed her against the wall, entering her deeply, her tortured eyes closing as she scraped her fingertips along his skin.

He was in love.

"*Eres mío*," Rose whispered confidently.

"And you, mine," Anthony replied.

Anthony treasured her and feared the day that she may leave him, worried that his deceit would destroy their relationship. As they lay together one night, their love evident in the sweat-drenched sheets and in the way their exhausted limbs hung over each other's bodies, he decided to tell her what he did for a living.

Rose lay quietly, her long, black hair loosely tied back off her neck and shoulders, while the humid heat of the night curled the shorter pieces around her nape and ears. Her plump body was delicately soft and kissed by the equator sun.

Anthony trailed his fingers down the side of her figure, deliberately touching her every curve. He stroked the soft roundness of her breast and the smooth firmness of her thighs. She lay with her eyes closed as she enjoyed his attention and affections. He felt the warmth of her skin along his sturdy chest, smelling her hair as its scent filled his senses.

"Rose?" he murmured.

"Mm-hmm," she replied sleepily.

"We need to talk."

Rose lifted her chin upward toward Anthony's face and propped herself up on her elbow. Her eyebrows wrinkled as she stared at him; her hand lay lightly on his chest.

"*Que?*" she asked. "What is it?"

Anthony looked into Rose's worried face. He loved her accent. The way she spoke, her w's sounded like v's. She was sweet and completely sexy; he hated to disappoint her.

"I want to explain to you what I do when I leave you, where I go for weeks at a time." Anthony paused, raising his arms over his head, flexing his muscles as he settled into his confession.

"Oh?" she replied. "I trust you Anthony, I need no explanation."

"Rose, have you ever heard of Mr. Garcia?" He watched her face, waiting for recognition. "He practically owns half of Guadalajara, and many of the small villages surrounding it."

"*Si, si,* of course," she confirmed. "He supports many. *Mi familia* also worked for him, many years ago."

"I also work for him." Anthony could feel his anxiousness rising in his chest, his heart pounding as he prepared himself to reveal the truth to Rose.

"*Si?* So...?" Rose moved her elbow out from underneath her, rolled over and covered Anthony's body with hers.

"So, I transport illegal substances into America, I work with horrible criminals and occasionally, I do despicable and horrifying things to people. I'm not proud, but it is unfortunately how I make my living. I'm sorry Rose...I'm sorry if this disappoints you. If you decide you never want to see me again, I completely understand. But I wanted you to know the truth."

Anthony wrapped his arms around her back and closed his eyes. He waited for her horrified response, for her to reject him, to say the words he had feared for so long.

Rose giggled, at first and then loud and forceful. "You think I will never want to see you again? *Por que?* Lots of *familia* work for Mr. Garcia. I comprehend the drug trade; it is how many make their living in Mexico. It is an honest living, for many will starve without it. I am very proud; you are a man who works hard," Rose declared. She brushed her lips across Anthony's chest as their eyes met briefly. Anthony sighed in relief as he grabbed Rose's bottom and pressed her against him, afraid that she may change her mind.

"You're incredible, Rose. I had no idea you were so open minded."

"You underestimate me, Anthony. Stop all this talk now. Come, let's take a shower. I need you, and it's *muy* hot." Rose climbed out of the bed, and Anthony admired her naked figure as she walked away from him, the beautiful outline of her curves beckoning him to join her.

Anthony smiled mischievously and hopped out of bed. He couldn't believe how lucky he was, how things in his life seemed to be going in all the right directions. Now that there were no secrets between them, he vowed to make Rose his wife, to claim her as his forever and to live the dream he had as a poor little boy, growing up in the projects of Boston. His dream was to have a wife, to have a family, and to have lots and lots of money.

He wished he knew then what he knew now, but his love for Rose was never a mistake. It was the only smart thing he had ever done in his life, and for it he was grateful.

# CHAPTER 10

*Lucy*

Jack rushed past Lucy for the front door, his pants half on, his shirt in his hand. "Wake the kids," he yelled as he cleared the porch and ran for his truck.

"Jack! I'm scared, Jack."

"Wake the kids and come to the house, Lucy. It's going to be all right, I promise."

Tears stung the back of her eyes and her hands trembled as she watched Jack pull out of their driveway, a cloud of dust following him as he made his way down the hill toward the main farmhouse. It wasn't until little Anna began tugging at her nightgown that Lucy realized she needed to move. This wasn't a time to be afraid and panicked; she needed to remain calm and strong for her family, for her children and for Jack.

Lucy grabbed Anna and swung her onto her hip, moving down the hallway toward the baby's room. Sammy still slept peacefully, his blanket pulled up to his face as he sucked on the corner of the abused and tattered fabric.

"Anna honey, we need to hurry and go to Pop Pop's house," Lucy whispered.

"What's wrong, Mama?"

"Pop's been hurt badly. Can you get dressed, sweetheart? Mama needs to hurry; we need to dress quickly."

"I can hurry," Anna stated proudly.

Lucy rushed into the bathroom and grabbed her hairbrush. She smoothed her hair back away from her face, tying it swiftly up off her neck. She glanced into the mirror and stared at her reflection. She could feel her eyes roll and her stare fade, becoming suddenly lost into a vague but familiar trance. She tried to fight the vision but her mind went numb with absence, her awareness compromised and beholden only to that which would appear in her subconscious. She saw Pop lying in a pool of blood, movement all around him, cries of disbelief and pain. He had been attacked, his life flashing before her eyes.

"Mama?" Anna called.

Lucy could hear Anna vaguely and tried to take herself out of the dream state. She tried to move her hands and brought them up to her face and touched her cheek. She tried to open her mouth, but her words were stunned and her voice quieted.

"*Mama*!" Anna screamed louder, and the sound of her daughter's panicked voice jolted Lucy to reply.

"One minute, Anna." Lucy bent over her bathroom sink, taking in deep breaths, as deep as she could while sweat beaded all around her forehead and upper lip. Pop was dying and her body was going into shock at what she just witnessed.

Lucy grabbed a cold, wet cloth and washed her face clean. She held on to the walls as she exited the bathroom, bent over. Lucy thought of Pop as she sunk to the cold wooden floor, the pain and grief overtaking her body. She felt weak and helpless. She prayed for the vision to be wrong,

She thought about Jack's pain, Susie Mae's and her children.

"Mama?" Anna stood over her mother, quietly rubbing her back as Lucy cried into her hands, the silent cry of a soul who had been punched in the gut, her breath gone and her inability to control her sobs bordering an asthma attack.

Anna started to cry. "Please Mama, what's wrong?"

Lucy raised her head and looked into her child's eyes. She felt a strong push on her back, almost a punch, but then she took a quick look behind her to reveal that there was no one. She had felt that presence before, the sharp touch and then nothing. She knew it was her departed mother's way of saying, "Get going. I'm here with you; I see what's happening. You need to move now."

Lucy climbed to standing and tried to calm her sobs so she could speak to Anna. She bent down. "I'm scared, Anna. Can you help Mama? Can you help me get dressed?"

Anna looked at Lucy, her big blue eyes tired and tearful. "Yes, Mama, " she replied. She took hold of Lucy's hand and started to pull her through the hallway. "First you need to put on your shoes." Anna's bossy little attitude took over as she talked to Lucy patiently, using her mother's own words against her, encouraging Lucy to get her clothes on.

"Then we'll get Sammy ready, Mama. I'll get his bag," Anna stated proudly.

Lucy dried her face once again and walked into Sammy's bedroom. She gently picked up his sleeping body and placed him into his car seat without disturbing him. She looked down at her fearless daughter who had harnessed herself with a diaper bag thrown across her shoulder. Lucy smiled; her daughter's ability to remain calm in a hopeless situation made Lucy proud.

Lucy grabbed Anna's hand and the car seat and together they walked outside toward the truck. As they made their way down the steps, Jack pulled haphazardly into the driveway.

Jack exited his vehicle, his hands and shirt covered with blood, his face still and expressionless as he moved toward Lucy. Lucy could see in his eyes the shock and acknowledgement of what she had already witnessed. Pop was dead—there was no doubt now.

"Jack," she whispered, her voice caught in her throat.

Jack reached for her; together they collapsed onto the front porch of their small farmhouse. They cried, their arms wrapped around each other tightly, words of confusion escaping Jack's mouth as sobs and disbelief enveloped them.

They held each other until their heads ached, until their eyes began to dry, and their sobs slowed and stopped. Their hearts were broken.

They sat quietly, staring out over the open fields and down toward the farmhouse where Pop's body lay, battered and lifeless. No words were spoken.

And then the eagle. Anna noticed it first, the eagle flying in circles, up and over the field; its wings were as wide as six feet, its flight as sharp and steady as an owl's. Strong and assertive, the eagle flew, closer and closer, entrancing them with its flight.

"Daddy, do you see that?" Anna pointed. Jack lifted his head and watched. Lucy placed her hand instinctively over Sammy as the eagle circled. She watched in wonder as Jack stood from his position on the stairs and placed his arms straight up into the air. The eagle circled ever more intimately, appearing to want to meet Jack's challenge, aggressively diving toward him and grazing his fingertips with its wings. Lucy felt the whisper of its flight against her face as it soared over her.

The eagle flew high up over Jack, back beyond the fields, and down toward Pop's farm, disappearing over the orchards. Lucy glanced back over at her husband as he closed his eyes, and a small smile appeared on his lips.

"What was that?" Anna asked.

"That was Pop," Lucy whispered. Anna smiled and her eyes sparkled as the sunlight reflected off Jack's truck, covering them with a warm stream of sunrise, blanketing and protecting them.

"Pop," Anna whispered.

She understood.

# CHAPTER 11

*Anthony*

One of Anthony's earliest memories as a child was that of his father's lunch pail. The black, steel box with shiny metal handle remained a fixture on Anthony's bookshelf for years. He remembered his mother packing his father's lunch at night so it would be ready for him when he would wake, before the sun would rise. He remembered his father's heavy work boots and how he would carry the lunch pail at his side, his legs long and strong, and his stature solid. Anthony was four when his father died, his memory undeveloped and skewed by the pictures his mother held on to for many years after, but he remembered that lunch pail fondly.

His father's death was an unfortunate event, an unforeseen accident that sent his mother and him into a spiral of uncertainty. Anthony's parents were modest people; his family lived on a middle-class income, his mother staying home to raise Anthony while his father worked long and hard hours.

After his father died, the decent to lower-class living was one his mother fought vigorously against, trying her best to hold on to the life they once had. After a year of struggle, she lost her footing and gave into the inevitable. They were broke. Anthony and his mother moved out of their conservative home, with its modest back yard and welcoming front porch and into a small apartment above a diner. Anthony's mother became a waitress at that diner, and life as they once knew it began to fade into their new reality.

At times as an adult, Anthony could still smell the food from that restaurant, the odor on his mother's clothing after working all day. Anthony's mother was proud and although she continued on after his father died, her eyes never sparkled again, and her smile never seemed to flatter her face as it once did, once upon a time.

But Anthony remembered being young. He remembered the lunch box and he kept it safe in his small bedroom where he would store all of his special items—precious things like the nickel he found on the sidewalk on his way home from school, and his father's thermos. As Anthony's memory of his father faded, his obsessive love for his lunch box prevailed. He kept it safely hidden under his bed, a folded picture of him and his father, tucked up under the lid of that box, its edges worn and wrinkled, evidence of the constant touch of a young boy who loved his father.

He saved the matchbox car he found while exploring the back alleys behind the restaurant where his mother waitressed. He remembered the day he found the small matchbox toy because he saw his mother taking the trash out to the dumpster. Anthony was eight at the time, worried that his mother would scold him for leaving the apartment while she worked. She couldn't afford a babysitter and he refused to sit in the diner all day, which was the only other alternative. Anthony promised her that he would stay put in the apartment, watch television, and do his homework. She reluctantly agreed, but if she caught him now playing in the alley, she would never trust him again.

Anthony ducked, hiding behind an abandoned vehicle along the side of the apartment building's brick walls. He held his breath as he watched her with caution, trying to remain silent and undetected. She made her way to the dumpster, tossing the overstuffed garbage bag up over its edge, then she turned back toward the restaurant. Her walk was sluggish; she stopped to rub the back of her calves. Her feet, Anthony recalled, were always sore and restless. She reached into her pocket and pulled out a pack of cigarettes. She lit one and inhaled the smoke deeply, leaning tiredly against the wall. She took her time.

The restaurant door opened suddenly, startling her. She threw the cigarette onto the ground and snuffed it out with her shoe.

"What are you doing, we have customers waiting for you!" the owner yelled.

"I'm so sorry, I just—"

"Hurry up. Get back to work!" The owner slammed the door.

She trudged her way toward the restaurant as if she were being dragged toward an existence that shouldn't be, a life that she never intended, a burden meant only for her and her heart and soul to carry. She opened the door then shut it, disappearing inside.

Anthony picked up a piece of metal and threw it across the alleyway. "Son of a bitch," he screamed into the air. It wasn't fair, the way she suffered. His mother wore her shame and loneliness on her face, the look of loss never quite fading from her expression. He hoped that someday he would hear joy escape from her throat again, that the unprovoked release of laughter he and his friends often enjoyed would find itself planted in his mother somehow. He wished that he were able to bring her the happiness that she needed.

Anthony vowed that he would take care of her someday when he was older. That he would have money, lots of it, and that she would no longer have to work and stand on her feet for the hours that she did. She would not have to sacrifice for him, and maybe she would smile again. Maybe there would be laughter.

67

Someday, Anthony would take good care of his mother.

# CHAPTER 12

## *Lucy*

Pop's death was a shock, the acceptance of which seemed to escape Jack and Lucy as they prepared themselves to overtake the farm and the responsibilities that lay within. Bombarded by her new obligations, Lucy busied herself with the organization of the finances and bills. She sat with Jack's grandmother, Susie Mae, for hours, discussing the farm income and the purchasing of supplies, her head spinning as they unraveled what they needed to accomplish to ensure that they ran the farm with the same competence as Pop did.

To make matters even more complicated, Jack had become obsessed with the investigation into Pop's death, the mystery of which baffled and confused law enforcement and infuriated Jack beyond reason. Lucy grew aware that her husband was becoming consumed by the idea of retribution. He had stockpiled ammunition and acquired additional gun supply. He climbed ladders and mounted cameras on all the barns and outbuildings. He would sit up at night and stare at the TV watching the footage, praying for a small clue, anything that could trigger his anger and give him an outlet for his pain.

After dinner and when daylight would start to fade, Jack and Charles would often escape to the old and abandoned gun range behind Mr. Nelson's fallen dairy barn, once used for the town-sponsored turkey shoot, now the location for meetings among certain townsmen, Jack and Charles included.

Jack's reluctance to talk about the meetings with his brother was worrying, his secrecy isolating from his wife. He continued to ignore her on most days, but she begged him to be an equal part of their marriage. "Please Jack, you can talk to me. I'm here for you, I want to help you." Lucy reached out her hand to him; she tried to touch him affectionately, but he pushed her away and stared absently outside the window. "We can't keep going on like this, Jack. I don't know what to do for you anymore."

"Those goddamn Mexicans," he muttered. He looked at her, straight through her as her eyes searched his.

"Jack, what are you talking about, the Mexicans?" Lucy could feel her chest heave, her heart heavy with sympathy for the Mexican families. She saw how families would come through town; she saw the hungry children and the look in their eyes. The farmers used the immigrant families; they put them to work in the fields and it seemed to her that it was a beneficial situation. Lucy was surprised at Jack's hostility toward them, for he had often used them in his own vineyard.

"Recently, an unsightly group of Mexicans had made their way through some of the local farms, their quality of work poor, and their motives questionable," he spat. "Mr. Nelson approached Pop just last week to warn him that the laborers were unruly and hard to wrangle."

"But that doesn't mean they killed Pop," Lucy argued.

Jack faced Lucy, his eyes eager for an explanation, for someone to blame.

"Who, then? Who would do this?" he argued.

Pop meant everything to Jack. Their once-animated conversations regarding the farm, personal and private conversations of family were all gone now. Pop was Jack's mentor, his hero in many ways, and his savior. They spent endless days and worked hard long hours together, a sense of pride and mutual respect always evident in the quality of their work. They loved each other and they loved the farm. The strong partnership between the two of them had catapulted their business into a tremendous success and source of honor for Jack.

Pop's death was a devastating loss and it was becoming obvious to Lucy that Jack was incapable of processing his pain. She watched him. The only person he seemed to confide in was Charles, and Lucy felt uneasy around her brother-in-law. Life had been disrupted and everything felt uncertain.

Pop was murdered. His body was found beaten—a fatal blow to his head with a blunt object the final cause of death. The person responsible for his death was still at large. Pop was a peaceful man; he had no enemies that Lucy knew of and he was a strong man. He should have had the strength to ward off an attacker. Perhaps there was more than one attacker. Perhaps he was caught off guard, or even targeted purposely, jumped from behind.

Lucy recalled sitting next to Susie Mae the day after the murder, holding her hand as she recounted her evening to the police, the last moments she spent with Pop and the events leading up to the discovery of his body.

"I had cleaned the final dish in the sink and Pop and I were talking about how wonderful the party was, what a great time we had, laughing about Charles and Kat and how we tried to surprise Pop with their visit. He kissed me on my cheek and then thanked me, convincing me that he truly was surprised. He appeared tired but he was happy. I laughed and hugged him tight, told him that I loved him and that we should go rest now and go to bed." Susie Mae looked up at the police officer and began nodding her head.

"We had a big mess to clean in the morning," she explained to him. Susie turned to Lucy. "I never should have left him."

Lucy could sense her guilt but urged Susie Mae to continue. "You didn't know what would happen, Susie. This wasn't your fault." Susie Mae wiped her tears with an old handkerchief that she clung to tightly.

"I kissed him again and then said goodnight. When I woke in the morning, I heard the horses in the barn making a ruckus that went on and on. At first, I thought that perhaps there was a critter in the barn, maybe a fox or raccoon that had found its way into the animal feed. I got out of bed and put on my bathrobe. I made my way through the house and toward the barn. As I walked across the kitchen floor, I noticed that Pop's door was ajar and I thought that perhaps he had beaten me to it. Maybe he had made his way to the barn before me. I continued outside looking for him." Susie turned to Lucy. "I should have stayed with him that night. He would still be here."

Tears fell from her eyes and her voice crackled with pain. She crumpled into her palms, sobbing, covering her face with her aging hands. She paused to catch her breath, and then she continued, "When I reached the barn, I slid the heavy door aside on its track. The horses quieted as I approached them; I placed my hand on Ginger, Jack's horse, and then I tried to assess what was causing my animals to act so chaotic. I walked across the floor and

73

rounded the corner toward the feed area…and that was when I saw him…laying lifeless on the barn floor, blood puddled all around him, his body hard and cold as if he lay like that all night." She gasped, descending into sobs once more. She reached for Jack, grabbing a hold of him for balance and then putting her forehead on his shoulder.

Lucy stood from her chair and walked across the kitchen floor to grab a glass of water for Jack's grandmother. Her eyes searched for Jack.

Lucy placed her hand on Jack's back and reached over to hand the glass of water into Susie's shaking hands. Jack placed his hands over his face and rubbed his eyes, then continued to look forward, his face unchanged, appearing confused still as he listened to her words.

Lucy began to cry, the vision of Pop too much to bear, the loss nauseating and unexpected. Jack stood from his chair, kicking it out from underneath him. "What are you people doing about this?" he screamed at the sheriff. "My grandfather is dead! Why are you still here asking questions? Go find the person who did this to my family!"

The sheriff stood away from Jack, startled by the sudden outburst of anger. "Settle down, Jack, we are doing the best we can.

The more information we have from Susie Mae, the better. I know this is very upsetting, but please, bear with us."

"What about the Mexicans?" Jack seethed.

"*Jack!*" Lucy stood, shocked at her husband's accusation.

"We're looking into that, sir," a rookie cop responded.

Lucy turned her attention to Jack, who seemed to be losing patience, his distaste over the entire interview process evident as he leaned over the kitchen counter, his hands on his face as if he were hiding his eyes from the truth.

"He was attacked from behind, hit several times in the head by a blunt object, causing him to fall forward and collapse into a pile of fresh cut hay," the sheriff stated.

Lucy stared at him with confusion. Why was he saying this now?

"We think the blunt object was perhaps some type of tool, a large tool heavy enough to crush a human skull in one single swipe." The officer approached Susie Mae and took her hands. "I am so sorry for your loss, ma'am. We are looking high and low to find those responsible for this, I promise you."

"Thank you, Sheriff."

The sheriff turned to Jack. He reached out his hand to shake his, but Jack refused. The sheriff stepped back from him and grabbed his hat off the kitchen table.

"Let's go," he said to the rookie standing in the back, and then they exited the house.

Jack stared out the kitchen window and watched them leave the driveway.

"Jack," Lucy started, "about the laborers, do you really think—"

"I don't think, I know."

Jack turned his back on Lucy and Susie and walked through the screen door, slamming it behind him.

Lucy turned to look at Susie Mae, who seemed to be struggling to stand, and raced to balance her and embrace her.

"Susie Mae, what are we going to do?" Lucy asked, her voice cracking as she fought to hold back her tears.

"Pray, baby. Pray for us all."

# CHAPTER 13

## *Charles*

The bar was crowded for an early Thursday afternoon. At quick glance, the patrons appeared joyous; the loud laughter was welcoming, like pulling up a chair and wanting to stay for a while appeared normal. But Charles knew better. He was socializing with some of the worst people: the hardcore drinkers, the farmers whose fields were left untended, the moms who put their children on the school bus then started their day with a drink at the bar. He was among them, attempting at best to fit in somewhere.

The bartender placed his drink in front of him—straight up whiskey, with a side of unwelcomed sarcasm. "We missed you yesterday. Good ol' Lance Wilcox was here all day, waiting for you. Says you owe him some money." The bartender wiped down the counter as he spoke, his eyes full of warning.

"Fuck Lance," Charles grumbled as he stared at his drink.

"I don't want any trouble here, Charles, you understand? Take that shit elsewhere. I'm not interested in the nonsense."

Charles stared up at the bartender—Jerry was his name, or was it Larry? He wondered if Larry knew or understand what Charles was capable of. Larry looked soft, like small town living didn't do him any favors. His frame was thin; his hands were smooth and untouched by hard physical labor. Farmers around here were tough as nails, strong, take-no-bullshit kind of guys. But not Larry. Charles could take him and Lance, if he needed to.

"You don't look good, Charles." Charles ignored the bartender, continued to stare at his drink. "I'm sorry to hear about your grandfather. How's Jack taking it?"

Charles narrowed his eyes in on Larry. He paused, then turned his swivel stool around and faced the front door, away from the bar. He was waiting for Christina, a young girl he had lots in common with. They shared the same desire to sit at a bar all day long, to do the drugs they preferred and occasionally, they had sex, something he and Kat never did anymore. Christina was hardcore; she preferred heroin to Charles' pain meds, her addiction obvious in the dark shadows under her once pretty blue eyes. She rejected everything normal, her family and friends. She was once a good mother, so she claimed, but the drugs destroyed her.

Charles convinced himself that he wasn't going to be like Christina. But the voice, the one that knew Charles was no good, echoed around his brain, claiming that he should be with his family, mourning his grandfather and helping his brother. He would, Charles would argue silently…but not today. Maybe tomorrow. Tomorrow he would be a better person, but today he needed to be with Christina; today he needed to feel nothing and to forget about his grandfather.

Charles and Kat had only been on the farm a short while but it felt like forever. It didn't take him long to find his people, the people who made him feel normal and accepted.

Charles tapped on his glass with his finger and motioned for the bartender to bring him another drink. Where the fuck was Christina? He didn't have all day; Kat would be a pain in the ass if he didn't show up at the house later. The clock on the wall showed 1:30. She said she'd be there by 1:00. Charles swallowed his drink and walked across the bar to the payphone. He dialed her house number. No answer. He hung up forcibly, shoving his fist in his pocket and removing a cigarette, nearly breaking it in half. He lit the crooked thing and stepped outside to smoke. Christina had what he needed, and she promised to meet him.

Charles walked up and down the bar's dirt driveway, pretending to admire the motorcycles lining the parking lot. His hands shook; he needed a fix. He watched as each car passed on the street, waiting anxiously. He smoked one cigarette after another.

Finally, she pulled in and Charles jumped in the vehicle.

"Hey," she said dryly.

Charles glanced over her way, his eyes dark, his mouth tight and unmoving.

"Oh what? You're not going to talk today?" Christina paused and stared at him for a minute, then continued driving, pulling around the building. She parked the car behind an old storage shed. She tossed him what he wanted and he grabbed it.

"You make this hard, Charles. A little personality goes a long way with me," she nagged.

Charles began crushing a pill on the dashboard. He took a one-dollar bill, rolled it then snorted the white dust up his nose. He sat back and waited for the warmth to flood his body. Christina placed the needle in her arm; her eyes rolled back in her head as her body began to relax. She tried speaking, but her words were slow and long. Charles rarely spoke when he was high—it was more peaceful that way. Besides, his mind was already actively telling him what a loser he was. He looked at Christina. She smiled cautiously, and reached out for him.

"I need money, Charles. Twenty dollars, I'll give you what you need." She swayed her words like music. Charles reached into his back pocket and pulled out a twenty. She snatched it and tucked it under her bag. She lifted her dirtied sundress and removed her panties slowly, dropping them to the floor. She slid across the front seat, unbuckled Charles' pants and pulled them down. Christina moved her body next to his, lowering herself onto him.

Charles reclined the seat and closed his eyes. He didn't want to see her hardened face or smell her nasty breath or listen to her stupid words. He wanted peace; he wanted to be away from the voice, away from his reality.

He could feel her moving on top of him, moaning as if she enjoyed what she did. He knew better. Her noise was distracting to him. Charles closed his eyes tighter, trying hard to block her and the noise in his head, but it was becoming impossible. She was so damn loud.

He opened his eyes to see her riding him and thumbing through his jean pockets. Charles grabbed her by the neck and threw her off of him, sending her flying across the seat and banging her head against the driver-side door. After she straightened herself, he smacked her again, sending a spray of blood onto the glass. This time she didn't move. Charles pulled his pants up, took his pills and his twenty-dollar bill, and walked away from the car.

He needed to get home. He was going to be late, and Kat was going to be pissed at him.

# CHAPTER 14

## *Anthony*

Anthony's motivation to be successful in life was entirely fueled by his need to give his mother the things that she had missed out on. He wanted to give her piece of mind, a nice home, and the security that they both missed after Anthony's father had died.

Anthony walked the halls of his empty home, imagining that he would turn a corner and see his mother standing there. He could feel her presence still; sometimes the shadows of the night moved unexplainably. He missed her. After she had died, Anthony seemed lost again. His responsibility to care for her was suddenly gone and he was careless and unsure where his life would lead him.

He picked up a framed picture his mother kept of his high-school graduation. He and several other boys crowded together, their arms draped casually over each other, their faces youthful and bright with excitement for the future ahead of them.

Anthony thought about Nicholas. The day Anthony met his childhood best friend was one he would never forget. Anthony was twelve years old and, as he did many times after a long day at school, he went out on the street, exploring the neighborhoods and getting into mild trouble. He had his bike and the $5 bill his mother would give him for emergencies, and he felt free.

He pedaled his bike all the way downtown, past the shoe cobbler's storefront and past Pete's barbershop on the corner. He made his way through busy intersections and over bridges and past St. Peter's Catholic Church up on 10th Street. He was heading south toward Jamaica Plains, a place where his father's old factory mill was located, where Anthony had spent many hours sitting near an oak tree, staring down at the men and women who came and went through the factory's gated front doors. The Boston Beer Company had an aura; the scent of stale beer was always in the air. Anthony felt close to his father here. He could imagine him walking down the sidewalk, his metal lunch pail at his side. He wished he could walk with him, hold his hand and they would talk important stuff.

Anthony sat staring into the space before him, thinking about his father, when he noticed something. A boy about his age stood tall on a graffitied concrete retaining wall. He watched him as he paced back and forth on the wall, balancing himself by occasionally lifting his arms and waving them from side to side. Anthony stood from the ground and jumped on his bike; he was curious yet careful not to disrupt what seemed to be a risky catwalk, one he may or may not be interested in making for himself.

Anthony stopped at the foot of the wall, behind which lay a mountainous hill marked with sporadic tree saplings and a line of rusty metal fencing. Next to it was a twenty-foot drop to the pavement of the abandoned parking lot. Anthony stood and stared as the boy continued across the wall, unfazed by the prospect of falling.

Anthony began his ascent up the hill, finding his way through a rugged, trampled path scattered along with gravel and an occasional boulder. He climbed through the twig-like trees, just big enough to be annoying, yet small enough to push aside, their branches scratching at Anthony as he climbed. He made his way to the top of the wall, glancing down behind him as he stood. It was high, higher than he anticipated; his heart beat from the physical exertion of the climb. He wiped at his brow, sweat beading on his forehead as he looked across the wall at the boy on the other side. The boy made his way across the top and sat in a small area of grass, folding his legs Indian style, as if he were ready to watch a cartoon show on the Saturday morning network. Anthony stared at the boy, not sure what to make of the situation, but was willing to try to make it to the other side to find out.

He stood on top of the beginning of the wall, holding on to a small branch brushing against his leg. He took a deep breath and placed one foot in front of the other. He tried to stare ahead, not wanting to look at the space between him and the ground below him. He moved forward, one step at a time. The sun beat down on Anthony's face, but a breeze cooled his skin as he tried to remain calm, trembling at the thought of falling. He held his arms straight out from his sides, as the other boy did, to balance himself. Anthony's stomach was tied in knots; the adrenaline pumping throughout his body made him feel alive. He was halfway when he noticed the concrete on the wall crumbling underneath his feet. The old stone, chipped away by water and weather, created another obstacle, making the endeavor even *more* dangerous and invigorating. He continued on, brushing away the loose stone with his foot and maintaining his balance by waving his arms like a wayward bird with great intensity.

He looked forward at the boy, whose dark hair appeared thick and sweaty from the afternoon heat. The boy had eyes that were dark and focused on Anthony's wall walk, eyes that looked relaxed and accomplished. A kindness settled into his smirk as he gazed toward Anthony.

Anthony continued forward. Only four steps to the end of the wall, and a sense of relief flooded throughout his body. He reached the other side, a smile of success stretching across his face as he leapt to the safety of the grass patch awaiting him.

The boy rose to his feet and jumped up and down with excitement.

"You did it!" he yelled. "You did it!"

"Did you see? I almost slipped on the concrete dust! Did you see all the stone that I kicked away? It was slippery. I almost fell. I can't believe I did it!"

"That was awesome! Hey, my name is Nicholas." Nicholas slung his arm around Anthony's shoulders to congratulate him.

"My name is Anthony." He grinned.

"Nice to meet you, Anthony."

"How do you get down from here?" Anthony asked as he looked around him for a marked path.

"You need to go across again."

Anthony looked at his new friend with wide eyes.

"I'm just kidding," Nicholas said as he laughed. "Come on, follow me. I'll get you down."

That was the first time in Anthony's young life that he had ever felt a natural bond, a companionship with a friend that felt real. Now, Anthony regretted so many things he had done in his life. His relationship with Nicholas had become a complicated one. But he smiled as he thought about him, a confident son of a bitch, even back then. Nicholas was definitely a friend.

# CHAPTER 15

*Jack*

It felt like he was a kid again, sitting in his childhood home living room, listening to the police officer explain to him that his mother was dead. He remembered staring at the officer, feeling like the officer didn't want to be there, that he would have preferred to be home already with his wife and kids and that this was a bit of an inconvenience to deal with these young, motherless boys.

Pop saved him. He was the only person in his life who had genuinely loved and supported him, made him into a man.

But Pop was gone now and Jack was spinning.

The pain caught Jack's breath in the morning, as he would drag himself out of his bed and into his pickup truck. He would drive himself to Pop's farm and pull into the driveway, imagining seeing his grandfather waiting for him with a steaming cup of hot coffee, like usual. It was like someone punched him in the gut every time he pulled into that driveway.

Sleep eluded him and he was lucky if he was able to rest a few hours each night. Jack was intent on finding and destroying his grandfather's killer. When he was young and his mother died, he did not have the means or the insight to be a man, to seek out his mother's murderer and seek revenge. He often dreamed about it, though. He envisioned how and when he would kill the man, beat him savagely into the ground until he no longer moved. He was older now; he understood more and he had the means now. Jack's fury was deep, for he had two scores to settle and he was not opposed to taking on old, pent-up anger and releasing it on whomever killed his grandfather. This was not going to go unchecked; the police were not doing their job. They annoyed Jack, as if Pop's murder was just a big inconvenience.

It had been known for some time that the local farmers utilized the illegal immigrants for the harvest season, and that those same farmers also hired the Mexicans to manage the odd farm jobs that the local tradesmen didn't have time for or required too much pay for. It was also no secret that Pop's farm sat on some highly sought-after real estate. Pop had been approached multiple times from high-end lawyers who claimed to represent the citizens of their town, and who claimed that eminent domain was an option, Pop's sale of his land was a reasonable decision. Big corporate conglomerates had their eyes on Pop's land, and Jack questioned whether they may have had anything to do with Pop's death. It was all very confusing and Jack was grateful for his brother.

Jack sat on the back porch, shotgun in hand. Lucy was struggling with the children—little Sammy screamed as she tried to get him to eat his dinner. He wanted to help her, he wanted to *feel* like helping her, but he didn't. The air was heavy, the pain still sharp in his chest. He imagined his grandfather alone, suffering strike after strike until he lost consciousness. He would have given anything to be there to help his grandfather, and to have been able to protect him. He shook his head and stared down toward the ground. It was his fault Pop died. He knew it. The poison of guilt filled his soul and the pain of it ached his heart and destroyed his pride.

Jack reached into his flannel jacket and grabbed his grandfather's silver flask. He opened the top and took a long swig of the golden alcohol. The fluid ran down the back of his tongue and stung his throat as he swallowed. Closing his eyes, he leaned back and enjoyed the bite as it landed sourly into his stomach where he suffered the urge to gag and vomit. He shuddered, shaking off the awful taste then placed the flask back into his shirt pocket.

Listening for his family one last time before grabbing his shotgun, he jumped down off the back porch and disappeared around the corner, making his way for the truck. There was a meeting with the guys to discuss what their next move would be. Life seemed to be moving in slow motion all around him and he needed to do something…he couldn't just sit around and wait.

He owed it to Pop. It was all he could do.

# CHAPTER 16

*Lucy*

Lucy unfolded a crisp tablecloth and lay it across her dining room table. She carried a stack of plates along with a handful of forks and knives and set everything down, grateful she didn't drop anything. She had arranged a lovely array of lilac as a centerpiece; her trees were in full bloom, the scent of which flooded her house every time someone opened a door. She went back to the stove and stirred the pasta.

It had been a few months since Pop had died. Kat and Charles had decided to extend their stay to help on the farm and Lucy had offered to cook them dinner. She hoped for a joyful meal, one they hadn't had in awhile. She hoped Jack would be in a good place today.

She glanced over at little Sammy as he crawled into the kitchen, his big blue eyes bright with mischief as he moved around, circling Lucy's legs and crawling across the floor.

"Anna honey, can you come play with your brother while Mama finishes dinner?"

Anna was a capable three-year-old. She walked into the room with a small book and Sammy's favorite rattle.

"Come on Sammy, look what I have for you. Come and get it," Anna teased. Sammy giggled and sat up as he stretched his arms toward his sister. Lucy walked around them, placing a pitcher of sweet tea and an unopened bottle of cabernet on the table. She set out several wine glasses and her white linen napkins. "Perfect!" Lucy looked over the table.

She walked into the bathroom and fixed herself up in the mirror. Jack would be home soon.

The phone rang.

Lucy hurriedly stepped over Sammy's scattered toys on the carpet and reached over the counter, knocking aside Jack's catalog of different vines and grape varieties that he had given to her earlier in the day.

"Hello," she said.

There was a pause on the phone.

"Lucy?"

"Yes?"

**94**

"It's Nick."

Lucy paused, her mouth ajar. She looked around the room nervously; she held the phone tight and walked away from her children for privacy. She glanced down at the farm. Jack's truck was still in the driveway.

"*Nick*!"

"I'm sorry to bother you. I know this is a surprise. Can you talk?"

"Yes, are you okay? Is there something wrong?"

"Sort of."

Nick cleared his throat over the phone; his commanding voice sounded exactly how she remembered.

"I was wondering…if you would consider doing a job for me. I could use your help."

He needed her. She knew he would call, her dreams indicated so.

Lucy walked around the kitchen, still glancing out the windows. Jack's truck was gone now. He was probably on his way home.

"I may only have a few minutes, Nick. What is it exactly?"

"My family is in danger. I'm looking for someone and I think you could help me find him. My home's been broken into, and I believe the men responsible are in Mexico. Your intuitive skills might be beneficial in trying to locate them. There's a decent financial reward, too. I hope you'll consider it."

Lucy was silent for a moment, thinking. "I don't know, Nick. I haven't done that type of work in awhile. I have different responsibilities now, with the farm and my children. I'm not sure if I could manage it. I'm not even sure I could help you."

She hadn't heard from him in five years. His voice though...she could never forget his voice.

"How's Beth, Nick? How are you?"

Nicholas let out a deep sigh. "I've been better." There was a pause on the other end. "Listen Lucy, I'm not going to lie to you. The job is dangerous. The men I'm looking for have been convicted of a series of crimes, drug trafficking and murder included. There is a certain level of risk that I want you to consider, but please realize I will be protecting you during your entire stay in Mexico."

She paused. "I need to think about this, Nick. I need to talk to Jack."

"Of course. We leave in a few days. I hope you can manage it. It would be nice to see you again."

Shots of excitement rang through Lucy's stomach as she listened to him. She bit onto her bottom lip, still in shock over his phone call and stunned by his request. A flood of emotion filled her; his voice stabbed her heart. She needed to say goodbye.

"I'll call you tomorrow, Nick."

Lucy hung up the phone. She hadn't worked in years. Her life had been consumed by the farm, the winery, her children, and Jack. Getting away from it all seemed unlikely, but appealing. She needed a break from Jack's hostile attitude toward her, and the state of depression they all seemed to be suffering from exhausted her. Perhaps it would change things up a bit and help everyone if she left for a few days.

She was interested. She was definitely interested.

She gazed at the kitchen wall, smiling to herself. She heard the front door open and snapped herself out of it.

"Mom! Dad's home," Anna yelled from the living room.

Lucy grabbed the fresh cut salad out of the refrigerator and put it on the table.

"Hey Jack."

Jack picked little Sammy up off the floor and placed him on his hip. Charles made his way toward the table and sat down. He grabbed the bottle of wine and opened it.

"How are you Charles, how was your day?" Lucy asked politely.

Charles smiled weakly and ignored her question. Jack looked at his brother and laughed.

"He just can't hang with me. The man's out of shape and we worked hard today."

Lucy offered Charles a sympathetic grin. "Well I made a great big meal; I hope you're both hungry. Where's Kat, Charles?"

"I'm here!" Kat announced as she walked through the front door, carrying an apple pie and a loaf of Italian bread. She handed her goods to Lucy and kissed her on the cheek.

"Thank you, Kat! This pie looks delicious."

Kat laughed. "It's just something I grabbed from the country store."

"Oh, Mrs. Tino makes the best pies," Jack replied as he joined Charles for a glass of wine. Lucy looked at Jack fondly, placing her hand on his shoulder as she walked by him. *Pleasant*, she thought.

Lucy placed a large bowl of pasta on the table. She helped Anna settle in at her seat and hoisted Sammy into his highchair.

"Did you get a chance to look at the catalog, Lucy?" Jack asked as he piled pasta high on his plate.

"I'm sorry, I didn't."

"It's important, Lucy."

"I know, Jack. I just didn't have time today. Besides, I haven't had a chance to go through our finances yet. I'm not even sure if we could afford the vines for the new orchard. Perhaps we should consider waiting another year. With Pop gone now and the extra expenses from the funeral and settling Pop's debts, I'm just not sure. The winery is about to break even. I'd like to see us make a profit next harvest."

Jack looked across the table at Lucy. His deep blue eyes penetrated hers, his face stern and serious. It seemed rare these days that he would support her on anything. Their relationship was stressed with Pop gone; they ran the farm and business together. They were partners and they worked well together in that way. She wished, though, that he would remember that she was also his wife, not just a business associate.

"So, let me get this straight," Charles chimed in. "The winery isn't even profitable yet?" Charles glanced at Kat, his eyebrows raised. He took a long sip of his wine.

"It's common, Charles, for a business to struggle in the first few years of operation. I'm not concerned by it. By my standards, I believe so far that the winery has been a huge success."

Jack laughed. "I guess we have different ideas about what success should look like."

Lucy stared at her husband. She took a deep breath. The level of patience she had for Jack was undoubtedly remarkable in moments like these, but his tone and negativity over the last few years was wearing her down. She reached for the wine across the table and filled her glass to the top. She took a sip and enjoyed the fruits of her labor as she swirled the red cabernet inside her mouth.

"Speaking of money, dear, I received a phone call today." Lucy looked across the table and watched as her family continued to enjoy their meal. "It was from Nicholas."

Kat dropped her fork with a clatter on her plate as Jack glanced her way. They all turned to look at Lucy.

"Well, this just got interesting," Charles commented.

Lucy rolled her eyes and ignored him. She sat tall and defiant, waiting for Jack's response. He remained quiet as he continued to eat his meal, ignoring her.

Kat stared at her sister.

"How is he?" Kat asked. "Charles and I saw him a few months ago, and he seemed very well. What is it that he wanted? Is everything okay, Lucy?"

"He wants me to work for him. It would be for a few days. Nick asked me for my help because his family is in danger."

Charles started to choke on his food and reached for a glass of water. Jack leaned back in his chair and continued to drink his wine.

"There's financial compensation, of course, and I think I'm going to do it."

Jack stood from his chair and kicked it out of his way. "There is *no way* that you are going to work for Nicholas. You can just forget it!"

Lucy stood up and faced her husband. "It's a job that pays very well, Jack, and you want your vines, so guess what? Now is our opportunity."

"The vines aren't that important, Lucy. You have other responsibilities."

Lucy walked around the table and faced her husband. "Please Jack, I need this. It would be good for me to work again. I would be proud to contribute something to the winery and to help you, financially. Please think about it. It's just a few days. Kat could stay with the children; you have Charles here to help you with the farm. It's the perfect time."

Lucy turned to Kat, her face desperate for Kat to voice her support.

"Yes, absolutely Lucy. I would love to watch the kids for a few days."

"Thank you, Kat."

Kat stared at Charles as she and Lucy waited for him to offer his support.

"I wouldn't let her go," Charles said. "You're fucking crazy, Jack, if you think she should go."

Kat reached over and covered Anna's little ears.

Jack shook his head no. "I'm not going to talk about this anymore." Jack turned and walked out of the house, slamming the front door as he left.

Lucy slumped down in her chair and looked at her sister. They stared at each other for a brief moment, then they both looked at Charles.

Kat mouthed her words softly. "You are an asshole."

Charles excused himself from the table. "Forget you two!" He walked out after Jack.

Kat reached over and grabbed Lucy's hand. "What are you going to do?"

"I'm going, Kat. I have to. I owe Nick. It's the least I could do."

# CHAPTER 17

*Lucy*

Lucy stepped out of the shower and onto the bath mat, water dripping down her body as she wrapped her bathrobe around her. She tied it and then bound her drenched, disheveled hair into the towel to dry. She gazed at herself in the mirror as she wiped the fog and moisture away from the glass, her reflection revealing wrinkles in her face. The dark circles under her eyes confirmed her lack of sleep. She wanted to make her family right again, yet everything was falling apart. She remained still as she listened to her breath move in and out; she counted the rhythm and calmed herself through her practiced mild meditation.

She thought about him, Nicholas, in times of weakness. She tried to forget, but the memories always came back, and she missed him. It was an unreasonable emotion, to miss someone she barely knew. But she did. There was a fondness about him, a nostalgia that felt familiar and comfortable. They held a special memory—at least it was special to her. He wanted to spend time with her, to take her on their first date, a romantic first date where perhaps he would have brought her flowers, and then taken her to dinner, just the two of them. He had shown her genuine interest and she had never felt that from anyone other than Jack. She wished she had kissed him all those years ago.

She wanted to see him again. Perhaps if she saw him, it would explain why she felt this way; it would confirm for her that he was the same person whom she had imagined—a good person, and a strong man. Or perhaps, it would confirm for her that he wasn't who she thought he was at all, that her feelings toward him were just a result of idle time, boredom naturally felt after years of marriage. She was instinctive, though. She knew he thought about her. She could feel it. The feelings were so strong at times that she was thankful for their distance. He was on one side of the country, she on the other.

The souls were struggling to set her straight, she knew. Her mother's spirit was screaming at her, not wanting her to lose all she had worked for, not wanting her to make the same mistakes her mother had once made. She questioned all these things and was acutely aware of the signs. They were against her, against this relationship. She wanted to ignore them.

Why was it so easy for her to miss Nicholas? She was married to a good man, a decent man. He took care of her; their children were happy. She was reasonably happy by most people's standards, but she felt helpless when it came to Jack. She didn't know how to talk to him and it didn't seem that he wanted her help.

Her intuition, she realized, was a source of struggle for her. She knew too much. She understood too much. Jack was a loving man, but there was something wrong between them. His childhood would always be a source of conflict for him, emotionally. He didn't trust her, at least not enough to confide in her, and she was frantic for the connection.

She remembered Nicholas fondly in these brief moments when she was alone, oftentimes when she was discouraged with her life and with her relationship with Jack. It was unfair to Jack how her thoughts would wander, but they calmed her. It was as if she imagined that there was someone else out there, someone who loved her just the same as Jack, perhaps even a little bit more, had she ever had the courage to find out. It made her feel special in a way that gave her confidence.

Lucy's unfaithful thoughts brought an unsettling fear and secrecy that she held deep within her chest. She allowed herself to feel things that were unimaginable, then punished herself for days, rarely acknowledging the thoughts, but disregarding them as foolishness brought on upon by idleness. Her guilt moved her forward and she would continue on and care for her family, but her instincts were strong and she realized that it wasn't just a coincidence that Nicholas' energy pulled her thoughts toward him.

Her decision to help him wouldn't go without sacrifice. Her cheeks flamed as she thought about this. She was deeply ashamed and scared of what may come of her and Nicholas, but she knew that she had no choice but to work with him again.

Lucy closed her eyes and imagined Nick's face. She remembered many things about him; mostly, she remembered how she felt when she was in his presence. She felt safe. She trusted him, unconditionally. She could see his eyes as they searched for hers; she imagined leaning in closer to him so she could smell his skin. What would have become of her life had she dated Nicholas instead of Jack? Maybe they would have fallen in love, maybe they would have married. She wondered if he could feel her somehow, know that he was still important to her. Nicholas had sacrificed for her sister, her family. His strength, his kindness, his courage...they would always mean something to her.

She could still hear his voice in the back of her mind, his words she could never forget.

"If you have any kind of feelings for me Lucy, I want you to consider them. Because I *do* have feelings for you," he had said, years before.

She thought about the job offer. She thought about Nicholas' plea for help, his voice strained but considerate. He was apologetic and reluctant in his request, but anxious for some assistance and guidance. He proclaimed that he had no choice but to reach out to her, and she believed him.

Her internal struggle was certainly matched by his, and Lucy's feelings were torn. Jack needed the money. Since Pop died, they had continued to struggle with the police to find answers and certain local members of the community weren't making it easy on them. The conspiracy against Pop and now the organized coalition to overtake his farm was wearing them thin and could destroy everything that they had worked so hard to build. Jack needed financial help to continue working the farm, to get them through this hardship and to keep the banks and the land savages at bay. For the first time, Lucy considered how great it would be to contribute something important to her family. The financial assistance would ease Jack's fears and stress regarding the farm's future. Perhaps it would lighten the load on their own relationship too, and they could go back to the business of being happy again. Maybe he would love her the way he used to, look at her with those eyes and make her feel safe again.

The job offer had risks, she understood. The sacrifice could be grand. First of all, her life could possibly be in jeopardy. The criminals Nicholas was searching for were dangerous. She had no doubt that Nicholas would do everything in his power to keep her safe. But Lucy was also concerned over of the emotional bond she secretly held for him, the tie to him she'd kept all these years, and that she may succumb to Nicholas in ways she'd only thought about in private. The ultimate sacrifice would be that her actions would jeopardize her relationship with Jack, destroying her family in a way that may never be repaired.

Then the feelings of guilt set in. She owed Nick her time. His need for her help was vital in his last attempt at saving his family, who apparently was in trouble. And Jack...she needed to help him. The voice in her mind was never clear on what she should do. But she was certain of one thing: doing nothing wasn't an option anymore. One way or another, something had to change.

She needed to help Nicholas. She knew that she could repay him for all he'd done for her. She also wanted to save the farm; she wanted to save her family, and Nicholas provided an alternate way out of their financial hardship. The money was grand, to be paid from the detective unit of the Boston Massachusetts Police Union. Secondly, there was a two-million dollar bounty awarded to anyone who could bring known narcotics dealer Mr. Garcia back to the United States for prosecution.

Lucy walked out of the bathroom. "I hope I'm making the right decision," she murmured to herself. She dressed and packed a small bag of personal belongings, then walked into the kitchen where Kat sat playing with Anna and Samuel. Kat turned, focusing on Lucy's bag in hand, her face desperate with concern.

"You're not going to Nick, are you? Please Lucy, you can't do this."

Lucy held up her hand, shaking her head no, stopping Kat's cry to convince Lucy to stay home.

"Lucy, I don't think this is a good idea. We can figure something out, Charles and me. We are here to help you and Jack. Charles has a little money saved…we can make this work."

Lucy spoke sternly. "We owe this to Nick, Kat. I know you believe that in your heart. All of our problems could be solved if I just do this one little job. Every part of me knows that I can help him."

"What about Jack? Does he know you've made your decision?"

Lucy rolled her eyes at her sister's question. "Of course not. He would never agree to this. I need to go now, while he's gone. Can you care for my children, Kat? Can you watch over them? I promise, I'll come home as soon as I can."

"Of course, Lucy. But I don't like this one bit. Jack is going to be furious."

"I'm sorry, Kat. We need the money. He's too stubborn to admit it, but he'll be glad when it's over and done with."

Lucy pushed past Kat and walked into the kitchen to kiss her children goodbye.

"Mama's going out now, Anna. I won't be back for a couple of days. Can you help Aunty Kat with Samuel? Can you be a big girl for Mama and be helpful?"

"Where are you going, Mama?" Anna asked as she placed her last puzzle piece in the correct spot on the board.

"Good job, Anna!" Lucy said with pride. Anna looked up at her mother and beamed, easily distracted by her mother's encouragement.

"Mama's going to work for a couple of days, but I'll be back soon. Okay, honey?"

"Okay Mama, I'll be helpful."

Lucy kissed Anna goodbye.

Kat pushed past Lucy and scooped little Anna up in her arms. "We are going to have the best time ever, aren't we?" she said.

Anna threw her arms around her and kissed her face. "Aunty, can you play puzzle with me one more time?"

Kat sat down next to Anna and smiled reluctantly, watching Lucy out of the corner of her eye.

Lucy bent down, kissed Samuel on his cheek, and squeezed him tight. "I love you Sammy, you be a good boy."

Sammy smiled, smacking his mother playfully in her face.

Lucy turned around and walked toward the door, tears gathering as she glanced back at her family.

"Be safe, Lucy," Kat said.

"I love you, Kat. Thank you."

Lucy walked out of the house, leaving her family behind, a prayer on her lips.

"Dear Lord, protect my family, keep them safe from harm and watch over them, always."

# CHAPTER 18

## *Nicholas*

Detective Nicholas sat in his seat as the Boeing 777 left the airspace of Boston's Logan International. He looked over at Alex, a non-flyer, a nervous non-flyer.

"You okay, Alex?"

"Don't talk to me."

Detective Alex had his eyes closed, his hands gripping his chair. His face was pale and his breathing was noticeably rapid.

"Come on man, it's not that bad."

Alex continued to sit stiffly, unable to move, unable to speak. Nicholas took out his laptop along with his file marked Anthony Massimo. He pulled out several pages and pictures of the victims and their families, some notes and paperwork to ready himself for the long flight. It wasn't a coincidence that Anthony

Massimo was released from prison and that his home was invaded all within the same week.

Nick tried to remember Anthony as a good person, but it was difficult. His childhood best friend had once been a strong companion, a stand-up guy with morals and principle. Had Nicholas been able to help him, things might have been different. The rapid infiltration of the drug trade into Boston and Philadelphia corrupted Anthony beyond repair. Anthony was once a respected carpenter, an established businessman with a sound construction company. He lost everything he had: his money, his dignity, and eventually he lost his freedom.

Mr. Garcia was to blame. His relationship and influence over Anthony at first seemed like a godsend. Garcia represented the respectable male role model that Anthony had always missed in his life, ever since his father had passed away. But that changed and Nicholas could see the relationship for what it was: a death sentence. Garcia, a known mobster and a wealthy, successful businessman, turned Anthony into a greedy, violent son of a bitch.

Anthony was finally convicted five years ago for transporting heroin in his private jet from Mexico to Philadelphia. The feds were able to capture him and lock him up, but not before an officer was killed during a violent shootout. Anthony's testimony against Garcia and plea deal with the feds shortened his prison time. Garcia disappeared into Mexico and hadn't been heard from since.

Nicholas shut the folder, disgusted with the criminal system, disgusted with his inability to stop the crime and violence.

The lights flicked on and off; the *Fasten Your Seatbelt* sign lit up above the seats.

A quick and sudden jerk of the plane sent Detective Nicholas' drink flying off his tray and onto the floor. Lightning flashed outside his window and rain poured down around the wings.

He looked over at Detective Alex. His head was down in between his legs, and his hands were placed over the back of his neck as he took deep breaths. Nicholas put his hand on his back.

"It's just a little turbulence, Alex, it will soon be over."

The plane jostled and jerked again, abrupt screams coming from some passengers. Nicholas look around him, suddenly feeling nervous and uncomfortable himself.

The plane continued to rumble and shake, and the pilot's voice came over the intercom to reassure the passengers that they would be fine, that they just needed to get through the storm.

Nicholas could see sweat pouring off Alex's forehead. Alex's hand was visibly shaking, his mouth wording the old school prayer that they all grew up on. "Our father, who art in heaven…"

The pilot came over the intercom again. "We'll be landing shortly, folks. We've seemed to pass through the storm. Sorry for any inconvenience." The passengers cheered.

Fifteen minutes later, the plane began a steady descent toward the runway, the turbulence over and the sights of the ground in front of them. As the plane landed, a sigh of relief and congratulations rang throughout the airbus. Detective Nicholas grabbed his bags and computer and followed Alex outside to the terminal.

Once on dry land, Alex turned to Nicholas, his smile bright, his shirt noticeably damp and wrinkled from the sweat and anxiety of his panic attack.

"I need a drink," he said as he wiped the sweat from his brow.

"You're a fucking pussy, man," Nicholas said. The two detectives shared a laugh. Nicholas placed his arm on Alex's shoulder. "Come on buddy, we've got work to do."

# CHAPTER 19

*Lucy*

Lucy paused in the driveway before leaving, glancing behind her, considering maybe she should say goodbye to Jack. Her walk slowed. What if something happened to her and she never saw him again? It was too late now. The tiny spark she felt for Nick and his job offer was exhilarating and nearly impossible for her to ignore. She was going to Mexico and she wasn't coming back, not until she had the money. The thought of never returning to her family was nonsense and Lucy pushed it out of her mind.

After traveling the six-hour flight, Lucy entered a small café adjacent to the private Mexican airport just north of Guadalajara. She looked at the paperwork Nicholas had sent to her via Federal Express in a manila envelope marked *Personal & Confidential*. She pulled out the sticky note posted to the top of her paperwork.

*Lucy, your help in this matter is greatly appreciated.*

*I look forward to working with you again, my friend.*

*Nicholas*

She glanced at herself across the counter in the wall-mounted mirror behind the coffee machine. She had been traveling all day; she was tired and couldn't wait to settle in her hotel room and take a shower. The details of her assignment were vague and Nick had said that he needed to explain them to her in person. She wished she wasn't nervous.

Lucy twirled her sugar spoon mindlessly around her cup of coffee and took a small bite out of a piece of pastry, hoping to calm her nerves while she waited for Nicholas to arrive. She sat in the swivel barstool at the counter, glancing around her. An elderly gentlemen sat to her right drinking his coffee black with shaky, tired hands. A few younger gentlemen sat to her left, eating a quick dinner, speaking in Spanish and staring at her occasionally. She realized she must have stuck out like a sore thumb.

She wanted to call Kat, to let her know that she was okay and to check on her children. She wanted to feel at ease; she was so nervous. She couldn't fix her hair one more time—she knew it was hopeless. Her appearance was not what she had envisioned when she imagined seeing Nicholas again for the first time, but there was no other way. She wondered when she spoke if her voice would

118

waver, if she were capable of holding a conversation with articulation. There was so much to think about—the assignment, Nicholas. The anticipation of arriving at her destination was stressful, so she thought a shot of brandy might help her, calm her nerves, and steady her thoughts.

The clock read 5:30 PM. Eyeing the walkway leading to the café, Lucy decided to stand and walk outside to get some fresh air. It was difficult to sit and wait. A few café patrons stared at her but she ignored their looks, knowing that she didn't belong. Her light skin and pale blue eyes were in stark contrast to that of the patrons in the restaurant. Her attire, her badly warn cowboy boots and lightweight summer dress, screamed farm girl and although that didn't seem so terribly out of the ordinary, she felt unprofessional. She smirked; she wasn't quite sure what an undercover medium was supposed to dress like anyway. She sighed; she was definitely too tired to sort it out.

Jack was going to kill her. This thought kept popping into her mind. She tried to explain to him before she left how she was feeling, her obligation to Nicholas and her need to work again, but Jack couldn't understand. He let his ego and jealousy rule his thought process and the discussion between them ended.

Lucy sat on a bench outside the café windows. She could see and hear the planes departing and arriving from the small airport. A crowd approached the café, a group of travelers. She looked through the crowd, eyeing every individual as they approached. Lucy recognized one man, she thought. He appeared to be looking at her as well.

She stood as he made his way, his smile confirming that yes, in fact, she did know him.

"Alex," she called and waved. Alex was Nicholas' partner; she had only met him once before.

"Lucy, how are you? How was your trip?" Alex grabbed Lucy's bag.

"It was fine. I'm a little tired, but I made it."

"Nicholas apologizes; he's a little held up. You can come with me; I have a car waiting for us."

"Thank you, Alex." Lucy followed him. He appeared more frazzled than she was and she wondered what kind of trouble she was about to get into.

"Hey Alex, do you know where I'll be staying? I have very little information from Nick and I hoped that I would be able to shower and maybe call my family at some point. To let them know that I'm safe."

Alex looked back at Lucy and gave her a steady stare. "You'll be safe, I promise you."

"Yes, I'm sure, but—"

Alex opened the door to the car and motioned for Lucy to get in. Once she was seated inside, Alex shut the door behind her and the driver moved away from the airport curb without him. She started to panic, but then a phone rang. Lucy looked down at the seat next to her and saw that there was a small cell phone vibrating on the black leather.

She looked at the driver, who stared at her from the rear view mirror.

She picked up the phone.

"Hello?"

"Welcome to Mexico, Lucy."

His voice stabbed her in her chest. Her senses were fully charged and on edge as her adrenaline ran throughout her body.

"Nick…" Everything was finally falling into place.

"I'm sorry I couldn't pick you up. Your driver will take you to your hotel. I left you some paperwork and a few personal items, a change of clothes and a case file. I need you to read through it, to familiarize yourself with the criminal outfit we are dealing with. Keep this phone on you at all times. Alex is with you; he will never leave you. You may not see him, but he is there, okay Lucy? Do you understand?"

"Yes Nicholas." Lucy paused; she was startled over the abruptness of her encounter with Alex and then the sudden swiftness of her departure from the airport. Thoughts swarmed her head, thoughts that she couldn't quite convey yet. Alex was with her, where? She looked out the back window and noticed another vehicle following them—a black SUV swerving in and out of the traffic. *That must be him*, she thought. She turned back around and looked at the driver, her hands gripping the cell phone she held, forgetting Nicholas was still on the line.

"Lucy, are you okay?"

Lucy swallowed hard, suddenly fearful for her life. "I've made a mistake, Nick. This is all wrong. I don't know that I could help you."

There was a great pause on the other line, a deep intake of air and then silence.

"Please Lucy, I need you."

Her heart broke; his voice was deep and meaningful, pleading with her, needing her. She felt suddenly responsible for him, his life and hers so different, yet he needed her, and perhaps she needed him too.

"Nick…I…I'm scared," she finally managed. Maybe she was in over her head.

"I know, Lucy. I promise you, I won't let anything happen to you."

His tone and authority always had a way of making Lucy feel safe. She was starting to feel calm again.

"I can't wait to see you," he said quietly. "Keep this phone on, got it?"

"Yes Nick, I will. When will I see you?"

"Soon, Lucy. Soon."

"I'm nervous, Nick. It's…been a long time." Lucy paused at her brutal honesty, hoping she didn't say the wrong thing.

"Don't be nervous. I'm grateful you agreed to help me. I'm looking forward to working with you again. We always made a good team."

There was another pause on the phone, and Lucy wondered what Nicholas was thinking. She clenched her hand into a fist and felt that her palms were perspiring. Her chest was hot and she could feel the back of her shirt sticking to the seat.

"Lucy, I have to spend the next few days trying to keep you safe, and you know keeping you safe is a full-time job that doesn't come without risk!" Nick laughed deeply, the teasing tone in his voice returning as laughter escaped him. The moment was lightened and relaxed, the seriousness of the situation ignored.

Lucy smiled. She remembered his seriousness. She also remembered how wonderful and rare it was to see him smile and be relaxed. She was grateful for this moment now, as it put her at ease completely.

"Stop it," she said with a chuckle. "I'll see you soon, Nicholas." Lucy spoke with a steadiness, a sense of stability starting to fill her.

"Thank you, Lucy."

"Good bye, Nicholas."

She hung up.

# CHAPTER 20

## *Kat*

Kat sat on the back porch of her sister's home watching Sammy sleep in his baby swing. Jack would soon be home and she was nervous. She was afraid of Jack's reaction, afraid to upset the children. She hoped to explain to Charles the situation and thought maybe she could take the children for a walk while Charles and Jack spoke. She didn't want Anna to worry about her mother; she didn't want the kids to think that there was something wrong.

Charles walked through the back door screen and dropped down onto the porch swing, sipping on his beer. He glanced down at his nephew and smiled at him, rocking the swing gently and leaning back into his chair. Kat watched him often with the children. She was grateful for this time she had with Lucy's family. It surprised her how Charles had taken to the kids, and she wondered if he would make a good father after all. Maybe that's what he needed—a family to complete him. He was attentive and concerned

125

and he seemed to enjoy the children. It seemed to be the only thing that made him happy.

"Anna," Charles called out to her. "Anna, do you see that?" Charles pointed up into the blue sky as a jetliner's wake streaked across it. Anna loved planes. She talked excitedly about taking a trip and flying in a plane with her uncle. She lifted her little head and glanced up toward the clouds, then pointed her finger and smiled thoughtfully.

"Where do you think they are going, Uncle?" she asked.

Charles stood and went to her; he kneeled down next to her and whispered, "I think they are going to see Mickey Mouse."

Anna's eyes went wide as she began to jump up and down, throwing her arms around her uncle's neck and grabbing at his face.

"Can we go, Uncle Charles? Can you take me sometime?"

Charles scooped Anna up into his arms and swung her around in a circle. "Absolutely. I can't wait to take you to Disney World. It will be so much fun, Anna."

"Today?"

Charles laughed as he put Anna back down on the ground.

"You don't miss a beat, not for one second, little Anna. Disney World is a far off place and we have to make a plan, buy

126

plane tickets, and make arrangements. We can't go today, honey, but we will someday, I promise."

Anna scrunched her disappointed face at his grownup explanation and decided to continue on her pursuit of the butterfly that had been eluding her.

Kat watched them interact. She loved Charles. He was adjusting to staying on the farm, being with his brother who relied on him and needed him now. Perhaps it was the guilt he had always talked about, how he had abandoned Jack when they were younger. Maybe now he would be able to reconcile those feelings and be a supportive unit in Jack's life. He rarely talked about the boat and going back to the East Coast. She wondered. Pop's death had opened an opportunity for him here. He was useful on the farm and it was obvious to Kat that he was beginning to assimilate to farm life.

Kat was hopeful. She was beginning to think about having children and it would be wonderful to be around her family, to be around Lucy and to watch the children grow. She looked at Charles differently now. She watched him with the kids, how gentle and protective he was of them. How Anna loved her Uncle Charles. It was sweet and heartwarming to watch this rugged man turn into a flying butterfly at the wish of a little girl. He was going to make a very attentive father, the opposite of the type of father he had growing up. Although he still drank more than she would like, Charles seemed happy, more so than she had ever seen him before.

But things were going to get ugly now. Things were going to be difficult for the next few days. Kat felt her nerves start to tingle as she rubbed her fingers over each other, a nervous habit she had as a kid, as she began to think about how she was going to break the news to Jack that Lucy had gone.

"Charles?" Charles glanced back at Kat with a mischievous smile and then made his way back to her, kissing her on her cheek while he took his seat again on the rocker.

"Why do you look so serious?" he asked.

Kat smiled weakly and then cleared her throat.

"Charles, Lucy's left. She took that job with Nicholas." Kat watched as Charles jumped back up to his feet and stood to face her.

"What the fuck, Kat?" Charles covered his mouth as he realized he spoke louder than he intended in front of the children.

"I couldn't stop her, Charles. I tried to talk her out of it. She feels so much responsibility. I didn't know what to do."

"Does Jack know?"

"No. I was hoping you could tell him. Perhaps I could take the kids out for a walk and you could talk to him. I don't want the kids to see him go ballistic."

"Oh my god Kat, what is Lucy doing?" Charles grabbed Kat by the shoulders. His pupils big and black, he stared at her. "She should have never taken that job. It's far too risky. Nicholas should have never asked her. I don't understand him."

"She wants to give Jack the money, for the farm."

Charles took a deep breath and stood away from the porch.

"You better get the kids going. Jack will be home soon. I'll talk to him. There's not much we can do about it now. It's too late, she's already gone."

"I know. I feel so helpless. I keep praying that this will all work out, but I have a bad feeling."

Charles stood on the edge of the porch, deep in concentration.

"I should go," Kat stated. "Anna honey, let's go for a walk and pick some flowers."

Anna smiled brightly. "Yay!" she screamed.

Kat left the house with the children and started her way down the driveway when Jack pulled in past them. They waved and continued.

Things were going to be ugly. She was not going to hurry back, she decided. She would go visit with Susie Mae until Jack calmed down. Maybe Susie Mae could reason with him. She hoped anyway.

# CHAPTER 21

*Lucy*

The driver pulled up toward the curb along side a moderate-looking hotel called La Hotel Villa. When he dropped Lucy off at the front entrance, she dragged her bag behind her as she walked into the reception area, pausing to look behind her, knowing Alex was with her somewhere. She thought about Nicholas again—he had told her not to worry, but she did. She felt alone and abandoned to some degree and she wasn't sure what she was supposed to be doing.

The hotel was lovely. Brightly colored tropical planters lined the walls of the reception area along with sporadic water fountains and comfortable chairs. The space was large and open with giant fans overhead making for a comfortable breeze in hot and humid atmosphere. Lucy approached the front desk, where a kind woman caught her eye, her smile bright and welcoming.

"*Hola, señorita,*" she said in a friendly manner. She moved from around the reception desk, took hold of Lucy by her arms, and greeted her with an affectionate hug. She appeared to have been expecting her. The short woman made Lucy feel at ease and comfortable in the foreign space.

"What is your name?" she asked as she waved for the bellhop to come take Lucy's luggage.

"Lucy Nimchak, ma'am. I believe I have a room waiting for me?" Lucy held her breath, hoping that the arrangements had been made on her behalf.

"*Si, si*, señorita Lucy."

The woman threaded her arm through Lucy's and walked her to a small staircase. She handed her a set of room keys. The young bellhop took Lucy's small bag of belongings and encouraged her to follow him up the stairs. Signs riddled the top of the wall directing the visitors. One sign had a picture of a pool with the word *Piscina* and an arrow pointing one way; another sign had a picture of a treadmill with *Gimnasio* pointing the opposite way.

Lucy said thank you to the kind woman and then followed the young man down the long hallway and around the corner, where he proceeded to put her bag down on the floor, waiting for her to open her door. She did and then she scrambled to find a few dollars in her pocket to give him, a tip for his help and time.

The boy excused himself while Lucy shut the door behind him, pausing for a moment and closing her eyes, thankful to be alone in her room. She was tired. She wanted to call home but decided she would wait until she had showered and slept. Feeling weak and fragile, she didn't want to convey her exhaustion over the phone to her sister, who would start to worry for her.

Her hotel room was quite comfortable and cozy. It didn't feel like a hotel room, but more like a guest bedroom in someone's home, with personal touches of material and brightly printed fabrics, real pictures of the town she was visiting, and fresh flowers in a vase on the small table near the bed.

She picked up the envelope Nicholas had left for her on the table. It was large and thick and she knew it would require a lot of reading. She wanted to have a clear head, a focused mind when she dove into it, for she knew that her intuition would be working over time and that a rested mind was often more controlled, less likely to wander. There was also a small shopping bag, which contained a few items of clothing that troubled her: a petit holster vest, a pair of thick knee-high socks that could also conceal a weapon, and an earpiece. She placed everything in the bag on the table and stared at the lot. She also took the phone Nicholas had given her and placed it beside the bag. She took a deep breath and then turned to empty her personal items in the small drawers next to her bed.

Sitting on the bed beside the table and leaning back against the pillows, Lucy closed her eyes. She thought about Nicholas and what her reaction would be when she finally saw him after all these years. She hoped to be unaffected by him, that her heart wouldn't race and that she would remain calm, and not nervous. But she was doubtful. She was *very* nervous. She could feel her anxiety slip away as she settled more comfortably into the bed, telling herself that she would only close her eyes for five minutes. She continued to fade away into a much-needed comfortable sleep.

It wasn't long before her mindless slumber soon turned into an unsettling dream, as she tossed and turned, struggling to rouse herself from her sleep. She dreamed she was in a place she recognized, the home she had made for her family. And Pop was there, sitting at her dining room table, laughing and raising his glass of beer, celebrating something with Jack. Everyone was laughing—everyone but her. She felt confused and watched as her family moved about her house happily, walking past her as if she was not there. She smiled at Pop; she wanted to hold him and to kiss his face.

"Pop! Pop! I can't believe it, you're here!" She went to him, but he turned his back on her. He continued on without her, unable to respond to her calls.

"Jack…I'm here. It's Lucy. Why is everyone ignoring me?" Lucy grabbed on to Jack's arm, pulling him, but he continued on

134

without her, lifting little Sammy high into the air and laughing at his smile.

Lucy stood still in her living room, watching her family enjoy their time together. Watching as life continued on without her. It would be a sad and lonely life she would have without her family. She moved, walking backward out of the home she had made for them. She could feel the tears streak down her cheeks, finding herself unwilling to accept the fact that she was no longer a part of their lives. She stumbled and caught herself, turned then ran down the porch steps out into the dark night and onto the stone driveway.

She continued to run, finding herself running in another place—a small town full of alleyways and side streets. She was being hunted; someone was chasing her. The dark shadows nipped at her heels as she ran. There was a panic in her. If she did not run fast enough, she would never see her children again; she would never see her family. She tried to scream, but no sound would escape her mouth. She closed her eyes and prayed, prayed for a second chance, prayed to make different choices. Church bells rang.

"Please heavenly father, forgive my sins!" she screamed.

Startled by the sound of her voice, Lucy lunged from her pillow and sat up; terrified, she was brought to her senses. Her phone was ringing, but it took her a few seconds to gather herself and to remember where she was. She slid off the bed and reached for the phone Nicholas had given her.

"Hello," she said quietly.

Silence. The phone went dead.

Lucy looked at herself in the mirror. Her hair was crazy, her eyes wild and dark. She was scared. She walked through her hotel room and turned on every light she could find. She glanced out of the windows, looking for something. Perhaps Alex was near, and she felt a small level of comfort, knowing that he may be with her.

She grabbed the phone again, sat down and stared at the device, willing Nicholas to call her, just so she could hear his voice. She waited for fifteen minutes, pacing up and down the hotel room, checking the phone regularly, but it never rang.

She decided to call Kat. She dialed her house number and prayed Jack wouldn't answer.

"Hello?" Kat said quietly.

"Hey, it's me. It's Lucy."

"Lucy! I've been waiting for you to call." Kat whispered, barely audible. "Are you okay?"

Lucy sat back down on the bed and breathed.

"Yeah, Kat. I just needed to hear your voice. I'm fine." Lucy closed her eyes and fought back her tears. She couldn't change anything now; she was in too deep and there was no turning back. She was a long way from home and she needed to finish what she had started.

"Tell me about the kids," Lucy implored. She listened as Kat chattered on about her children, reassuring Lucy that they were in good hands and that she needn't worry about them. Slowly, Lucy could feel her anxiety slip away as a certain level of bravery resurfaced, shaking off that horrible dream.

She said goodbye to Kat, told her she loved her, and hung up the phone.

She hopped into the shower and waited for the water to warm. She leaned against the wall and closed her eyes. She was tired of feeling uncertain, tired of being confused.

"I refuse to be scared," she stated, then let the warm, comforting water splash against her face.

# CHAPTER 22

## *Lucy*

The next morning brought rain. Tropical downpours sheeted the windows as Lucy stared out of her hotel room and looked down at the streets below her. She could see her soft reflection in the glass as the water rained down. She wasn't prepared for the storm, but perhaps the hotel had an umbrella she could borrow. She stood against the window and let the calming flow of water meditate her. She thought about Nicholas.

It was still warm and damp. She decided to wear a simple pair of old jeans and a casual top—pretty yet functional. She pulled her hair back and threw on her worn-in boots and tattered cowgirl hat. She glanced at herself in the mirror. She took a deep breath, anticipating that she would soon see Nicholas and that many of her questions would be answered. Her dream last night worried her, but she shook it off and decided that it was just a dream, not a premonition.

She heard a knock on the door—maybe it was finally him. She walked across her hotel room and opened the door, but it was just the bellhop from the night before, apologizing for interrupting her. He informed her that a car was waiting for her, when she was ready. Lucy turned, grabbed her phone, and followed the bellhop down the stairs. She walked hurriedly through the reception area while the bellhop ran after her, trying to open an umbrella to protect her against the pouring rain. Lucy hopped into the car and shut the door, listening to the young boy exclaim to her, "Please ma'am, take this umbrella." Lucy rolled down the window and grabbed the wet fabric while the car driver pulled away from the curb.

"Thank you!" she yelled from inside the vehicle.

She sat back against the leather seat and took her wet hat off her head. She was grateful for the protection it offered, and was content in accepting the fact that today was going to be a bad hair day. She held on to Nick's phone, anxious. She wanted to hear his voice again. She wanted to feel the comfort of his strength and confidence. She looked at the phone several times and opened it to be sure that it was functioning properly. She sighed. She wondered where she was headed to, what she was going to do next.

She had spent the entire morning reading through the police files on a Mr. Garcia and Anthony Massimo. She had a list of questions for Nicholas, and an overwhelming feeling that he was somehow connected to Anthony. Garcia and Anthony were involved in importing drugs into the United States—that was very clear. Nicholas had been watching and following the two for six months, investigating them for drug trafficking when he finally had a break in the case. Twenty million dollars of cocaine were seized. It was the biggest drug bust in Nicholas' career, but not before Garcia shot and killed a police officer, then disappeared without a trace. Anthony was arrested and agreed to testify against Garcia, reducing his prison term to only five years, but the authorities were never able to apprehend Garcia for his crimes. Garcia had a warrant out for his arrest, wanted for questioning on a multitude of offenses, murders, and questionable legal contracting deals.

Reading about Mr. Garcia made her stomach nauseous. She could feel the sadness in the pictures that she stared at. It sent shivers throughout her body; he was a very hated man. She understood why Nicholas wanted them. His home was broken into, coinciding with the fact that Anthony had just been released from prison. Nicholas was a threat to both of them and they were a threat to him. He was the lead detective in the case and had cost Garcia a ton of money along with Anthony's life in prison. Lucy suspected that it never sat well with Nick, that the case was never closed and that Garcia was never brought to justice. She figured Nicholas hoped that Anthony would lead him straight to Garcia.

Lucy looked out of the vehicle as they passed through town. She saw small glimpses of the marina as she glanced down the alleyways and between buildings. The falling rain pattered against the top of the vehicle. She looked up ahead and noticed that they were heading out of town and up into the mountains of Chapala. A layer of thin clouds lingered in the steep hills, leaving her with an eerie and unsettled feeling. The winding road was narrow and sharp as they passed small farms on the way; goats and cattle were scattered throughout the fields. The driver continued forward until he came along a hidden driveway. Had Lucy been driving, she would have never noticed the entrance entangled with palm trees and a canopy of rainforest vines.

They continued up another winding, cobblestone road until they came across a large barn overlooking fields of pasture that reminded her of her own farm.

The driver stopped the vehicle and then turned and glanced at Lucy, nodding his head in encouragement for her to go on without him. Lucy grabbed her umbrella, opened it and then pulled her hat on top of her head. The rain was still coming down hard as she ran across the driveway toward the barn's entrance. She hopped over the large puddles that had formed over the stone and she stood and waited in front of the door. It opened suddenly as she was pulled inside, away from the pouring rain.

Four Mexicans stood inside the building, staring at her. She was almost about to scream when she heard Alex's voice come from behind her.

"It's okay Lucy, they are with us."

Lucy turned to face Alex, her anger starting to get the best of her. She didn't quite understand why all the secrecy.

"Where is Nicholas, Alex? I want to see him. Where are we? Why is this all so secretive? I think you people are all acting crazy!"

"Alright, calm down, calm down. I'll explain some things to you, and Nick will be here shortly."

"What the hell, Alex? I didn't agree to all this. I thought I was brought here to help. But so far, I don't know where I am, Nick is missing, and I don't even know what the hell is going on!"

Lucy looked at Alex. His eyes were full of understanding and his face softening as he listened to her panic. He had a pleasant way about him, and when he smiled at her, she couldn't help but feel a little foolish for yelling at him.

"Carlos, grab Lucy a cup of coffee and meet us in the room at the back of the barn." Alex looked at the other men and nodded toward them. "Boys, you know what is expected of you."

Lucy watched as the men, fully armed with rifles, turned and exited the building. The men were of various sizes: one tall, one short, one round and friendly. They were dressed like ordinary farmers—jeans, boots and vests lined with additional small handguns and pocketknives. Lucy felt her outfit was appropriate and that she fit right in except for the arsenal of weapons that they had over her. She had a worrying feeling, however, that this was about to change.

Lucy followed Alex through the large abandoned barn. Although it was currently empty, at one time it seemed to house cows. She could recognize the smell of cow manure anywhere. The barn was typical, other than its overwhelming size. It was one of the biggest barns she had ever been in, bigger than Pop's. Some of the roofing seemed in disrepair and she could see and hear the rain coming in from the outside.

She followed Alex past the abandoned stalls, some still loaded with hay and materials and leftover forks and shovels.

He turned around frequently to see that she was following and to smile that everything was fine. She trusted him. She knew that Nicholas thought highly of Alex, and she was starting to see why. He was a caretaker. Nicholas probably needed a caretaker, someone who had his back, regardless of how dangerous a situation was. Nick and Alex had been partners a long time. She wondered if Alex was married or if he had any children.

Lucy turned around and noticed Carlos was also following them with what seemed to be a thermos with paper cups, the coffee Alex had asked for. It seemed strange to her to have someone else serving her coffee, but after her damp morning, she was looking forward to it.

Alex began the descent down a small flight of stairs, eight steps in total and then down a narrow hallway that ran underneath the barn floorboards toward the back of the building. She followed him closely, taking in the architecture of the building, the layout of the passageways and the old tracks that lay beneath her feet, the old-school methods of passing materials between buildings. The ceiling was short, and Lucy walked with her head down as they passed through, not wanting to hit her head or disrupt the old set of cobwebs that lined the ceiling and the walls.

After a few more quick turns around a corner, they came upon the back room that Alex had spoken of. Alex knocked three times and then the door opened. Another man stood on the other side, looking first for Alex and then glancing down the path toward Carlos and Lucy. He opened the door to let them inside. Alex turned before Lucy entered, stating, "Don't get upset now. What you're about to see may be unsettling to you, but keep it together."

Lucy had been clutching her fists so hard that her nails dug into her skin. She was sweating, unable to control her nervous reaction. The excessive heat and humidity wasn't helping.

She entered the room. She had seen dead bodies before. She had been a part of a criminal investigation where three people had been murdered. She felt that she had been desensitized to what it was she may be witness to, but this was different.

It was a very large room with three tables placed in the middle, big enough to sit ten, maybe twelve people each. The room was packed with an arsenal large enough to fuel a small army, an army big enough to invade a medium-sized village and kill thousands of people. The gun supply racks lined every inch of wall space available. Machine guns, shotguns, handguns—every kind of gun imaginable. As she walked into the room, her mouth opened as she looked up and down the walls. Several men sitting at a table playing cards turned to look at her.

She was amazed at what she saw. Her eyes met Alex's as he stood near her, watching her, seeming to wonder what it was she was thinking. The three men who sat at the tables stood up and approached her. Carlos poured her a small cup of coffee and handed it to her.

Alex spoke. "Carlos, this is Lucy. Lucy, this is Tony, Miguel, and Diego."

The men nodded at her.

"Lucy is a medium; she's here to help us. She has a special gift that we hope will be beneficial to our quest to find Mr. Garcia."

The men nodded as they looked at each other in understanding. Lucy was still confused.

"Lucy, as you know, I am a United States citizen. I work as a detective in the great city of Boston. I'm proud of my country and I follow the laws that lay there within. But here, Lucy, here in Mexico, we are only visitors, sent here with American passports. Our professions mean nothing and our status with the local police force means even less."

Lucy stared at Alex as he spoke. She understood: They were on their own here. There would be no legal help from anyone, other than the men who stared at her. They were searching for two very powerful and dangerous men, Mr. Garcia and Anthony Massimo.

"We are vigilante, Lucy. This is our only way."

There was that word. "Vigilante."

She understood.

# CHAPTER 23

## *Jack*

Jack slammed the front screen door open and jumped down off the porch. Charles was two feet behind him, yelling, "Jack, hold on a minute. Let me explain some things. Please, Jack."

"Fuck you, Charles. I've heard enough out of you." Jack flung his truck door open, hopped inside, and started it.

"Wait, Jack." Charles grabbed hold of the passenger door. Charles managed to jump into the truck as Jack slammed his foot on the gas pedal, reversing out of his driveway then flying up the road heading toward Kat.

"Jack, please let me explain. She thinks she's helping you. She thinks she's doing you a favor. We *do* need the money. Why don't you let her be helpful? Perhaps she could set us straight with the farm."

"Who's us? The farm was Pop's farm. I've been working this land with him for over fifteen years now. There is no 'us,' Charles. It's just me, and forgive me if I don't want my wife out on some wild goose chase with an old boyfriend of hers in some far-off place. I don't even know where she is. How could Kat let her walk away like that? I don't understand."

Jack's truck made it up past the cornfield and along the edge of the lower pond. Squirrels ran in and out of the road, scampering back and forth like moving targets, narrowly escaping death by jumping back toward the tall grass along the tree line.

Jack could see Kat up ahead walking with his children, heading straight for him. Jack slowed his vehicle to a stop and jumped out of his truck. Kat halted where she was and bent down to whisper into little Anna's ear, keeping her eyes keenly on Jack.

Kat stepped away from Anna to meet Jack in the road, and glancing back behind her, she spoke. "Stay there, Anna. Keep an eye on Sammy while I talk to Daddy, okay?"

Kat looked toward Jack as he approached her with rapid urgency, his heavy boots crunching the stone gravel. He grabbed her arm and pulled her close to him so she could hear him clearly.

"What the hell were you thinking, letting her go like that? What do you think will happen if she never comes home? I swear, Kat, if something terrible happens to her, this will be all your fault."

Jack snarled into Kat's face as he spoke, his neck red with anger as his grip continued to squeeze her. "Look at those kids over there. Who do you think will care for them if something should happen to their mother?" Jack could see the fear in Kat's eyes and realized that his fingers were ripping into Kat a little stronger than he intended. He reluctantly let her go, watching her retreat a few feet away from him, rubbing her arm.

"Jack, I tried to stop her. I tried. She wasn't going to listen to me." Kat's voice started to break as tears fell from her eyes. Charles was by her side as he put his arm around her; he walked her back toward the children, who were still standing on the side of the road, looking nervously at the adults.

"You're taking this out on the wrong people, Jack. We don't control your wife," Charles spat as they walked away.

Jack narrowed his eyes in on his brother and then turned and stalked back to his truck. He hopped inside and sped off past Charles, Kat, and the children, making his way toward town. He went over it in his head, over and over again. The fact that Lucy was with Nicholas created a firestorm within him. He knew his jealousy had a grip on him, but he couldn't help remembering that Nicholas had been in love with Lucy years before.

Jack couldn't believe she disobeyed him. He thought he made himself very clear to her—he did not want her to go. Perhaps it was innocent and that Nicholas did need her help, but he would have never agreed to this meeting. He didn't care about the money. He would find it somehow. He felt horrible for the way he had been treating Lucy. He knew that he had been under a lot of stress, trying to focus on taking care of the farm and trying to find Pop's murderer. He had been so angry. Perhaps she just wanted to relieve Jack of the stress of finances. He knew that she was sweet like that—naïve but sweet.

Nicholas. He couldn't be trusted.

Jack pulled over at the local country store and walked inside. The owner, Mr. Jenkins, said hello but Jack was so focused on what he was doing, he didn't hear him. He walked toward the back of the building and grabbed a bottle of whiskey off the shelf along with a pack of cigarettes. He threw a twenty-dollar bill on the counter and hustled out of the store without saying a word.

He drove up past Pop's farm toward the shooting range, where he parked his truck to think about what he wanted to do. He opened the bottle of whiskey and let the brown liquid burn down his throat. He shuddered as the harsh alcohol hit his stomach, feeling the poison mix with his lunch. He wanted to go to his wife. He wanted to find Lucy, but he couldn't. He couldn't just leave the farm, and all the responsibilities and obligations. There was too much at risk.

Jack leaned his head back and closed his eyes. He took another swig of the alcohol, feeling overwhelmed. He had no control over anything anymore. He could feel his frustrations eating away at his flesh. He needed a release; he needed to relieve the pain that he was in, but he was unsure how.

So he drank.

He drank until he felt nothing for no one, his vision vague, the noises he heard muted and unreal. He could feel his tears fall from his eyes and onto his face, but he no longer could lift his arm to wipe them.

He was a man, but his chest burned with hurt and his reality was beginning to defeat him.

# CHAPTER 24

*Lucy*

Lucy sat at the table with the five men, their eyes piercing hers as they spread out pictures and paperwork, all in chronological order for her to inspect. She cleared her throat and glanced at the men's faces. They waited for her to speak, as if her words were somehow divine intervention. The pressure was intense and although she had already looked over the notes and photos Nicholas had left her, the feeling in the room was incredibly heavy.

Lucy realized that these men were vested. Carlos, who sat closest to her, pulled on her heart the most. Lucy leaned into him and whispered, "There's a female presence here; she stands behind you with her hands on your shoulders."

Carlos stood and looked behind him, startled by Lucy's comment. Lucy grabbed his hand and pulled him back down next to her.

"She enjoys when you play the guitar to the children. She sits close and she listens. The children smile at you; their spirit awakens to the music. It helps them."

Carlos lowered his head and closed his eyes. His lips quivered as he tried to control his emotions. Lucy was not sure she should continue and turned to Miguel, who was sitting to her right. Her eyes pled with his; she needed some confirmation of what she was seeing in order to continue.

Miguel leaned in. "Miss Lucy, Carlos' wife recently passed away. He has three children he cares for. We believe she was murdered, shot cold blooded while she sat in her car awaiting her daughter in the school parking lot."

Lucy slouched down into her chair. Overwhelmed, she covered her mouth with her hand. She placed her other hand on Carlos', squeezing as he remained still and quiet.

"Have you all suffered? Have you all lost a loved one? Is Garcia responsible?" Lucy asked tearfully.

"*Sí*," Miguel responded first. "Diego lost his whole farm. Garcia's men burned the buildings down to the ground and tore through the harvest, shooting any animal or thing that crossed their way."

"*Si*, and *su madre*, she is forced to work for him. Like a slave she works, with no compensation," stated Diego.

"But why?" Lucy asked.

"We fight Garcia and his gangs. We fight for what's right and we try to save and protect those who are weaker than him."

Lucy nodded her head in understanding.

"But we pay a price. Everyone here has paid a price."

Lucy took a deep breath. She looked down at the paperwork and the photos in front of her. She moved her hands over the pictures and closed her eyes. She could feel heat penetrate the palms of her hands and move up and down her arms. The bloodshed was frightening and the suffering was immense. "Garcia is coming tonight. He's coming for Anthony."

The men looked up at her. "Are you sure?" Miguel asked.

"Yes I'm sure. He will be here, in town. Tonight's the night."

The men started to stand and move around the room. They removed guns from the walls and began placing them onto the tables, inspecting their condition and ammo supply. Lucy leaned into Carlos and wrapped her arm around him gently. "Are you okay?" she asked quietly.

"I play guitar every night for my children," he stated with a smile. "She watches us. It is a very good sign, very good, Miss Lucy." He stood and immediately got to work on arming Lucy with the appropriate gear and apparatus, so she could protect herself and to keep safe from any violence that may come her way.

"Do I really need all of this?" Lucy asked, startled by the sudden attention. "Perhaps I can just wait back at the hotel while you all work this out." Lucy chewed on her fingernails, concerned as the men continued to move all around her, ignoring her as she spoke. Carlos was her main go-to guy; he seemed to understand the most English and seemed genuinely worried for her safety. He explained to her the features of the small shotgun that he thought would appropriately fit her shape and size.

Lucy was no stranger to guns, even though Nicholas had never let her carry one in Boston during the investigation of her sister's disappearance. Jack had thought Lucy should learn how to shoot a shotgun a long time ago. He felt that if she had been riding out in the wilderness and if she happened upon a wild animal of sorts, she better know how to shoot it. Pop was adamant about that too. Even Susie Mae was shotgun savvy.

She tried to explain this to Carlos, but he refused to listen to her. He needed to see for himself. He and Alex led Lucy to the indoor shooting range. The shooting range was rustic with a backyard kind of appeal: An uneven dirt floor lay beneath them and a low ceiling of plank board was above them, creating an enclosed feeling, almost like an underground cave. At the far end of the room sat a small bench littered with old beer cans and soda pop bottles. She turned back toward Alex and Carlos and smiled. "Really, guys?"

She chuckled as she approached the counter, standing with her weapon drawn and her legs spread wide to steady her. The shotgun was a little bit larger than the one she had at home but she could manage it. Carlos handed her the slugs and watched her while she loaded her weapon. She knew she was being tested, so she double-checked and unlocked the safety, loaded her weapon and then pumped it once just for dramatics. Carlos handed her a set of earmuffs, but she refused to put them on. She would never be wearing earmuffs in an emergency. Why should she wear them now?

Carlos seemed to accept this without argument as Alex and he took a few steps behind her, watching her as she readied herself. She stood at the counter, taking in a deep breath, aiming her gun at the middle glass bottle. She pulled the trigger. The impact of the shot rammed the gun against her shoulder, causing her to yell out in pain as she jolted backward, almost tripping as she fell down against a strong body of someone she hadn't been expecting.

It was Nicholas.

She slammed into him so hard that she felt his feet stumble for a moment, but then he lifted her off the floor and into a standing position, grabbing her weapon and steadying her.

"Nick!" she exclaimed.

Nick did not look happy to see her. He turned and faced Alex and the two men standing there.

"Alex! What the hell are you guys doing here? Are you trying to get her killed? This gun is far too big for her."

Lucy watched as the men squirmed, trying to defend their actions and to convince Nick that this wasn't a big deal, that she was fine and that she didn't get hurt. Carlos stated several times that she'd done this before, that he was confident she could handle the gun. "She just needs a little practice."

Lucy stood tall and approached Nicholas. "Please Nick, hand me the shotgun. I was just a little taken aback by its power, but now I know what to expect. I can do better," she stated firmly.

Nicholas glanced at Lucy, his face still angry and firm. Lucy smiled and touched his shoulder as she took the weapon from his hand. She turned around again and walked back to the countertop.

"Carlos?" she called.

Carlos was soon next to her with the slugs she needed and a whisper of encouragement, soft enough that only Lucy could hear.

"Hold strong, Miss Lucy. Use your arms to steady."

"Thank you, Carlos." Lucy took a deep breath and steadied her hands. She loaded the gun and cocked it. She closed her eyes and prayed for the strength to stabilize herself. This may be her last chance with Nicholas to get it right. He may or may not decide to let her carry a weapon after all—and she definitely needed one.

Lucy raised the gun and aimed it at the middle Coke bottle. She looked between the barrels and lined up perfectly with her target. She pulled the trigger.

Again, she was jolted backward, but this time she was able to recover and she didn't lose her footing. She hit her target with ease, then turned back and smiled at Nicholas.

"Well done, Lucy. Not bad," he stated. Nicholas turned and addressed Alex and Carlos. "Boys, bring me the rifle now. She's going to need a real weapon."

Alex and Carlos left the room. Lucy stood still, staring at Nick, proud that she had impressed him enough to graduate to a bigger and better gun. She stood there watching him, waiting for him to say something to her, something to break the silence between them. She was almost certain that he could hear her chest

158

pounding, that the redness and heat of her cheeks was a clear giveaway that she was nervous around him.

He looked the same. His voice was exactly how she remembered it. His eyes were keen and sharp, the way he stared back at her, as if they both needed to take each other in.

No words were needed.

Lucy waited; she didn't want to be the first one to begin. Where would she begin, anyway?

A grin spread across his face. His smile melted her heart because it was rare, she knew. The seriousness of his nature was always evident in his face, although he was soft and caring underneath. She smiled right back at him, then took two feet forward and he embraced her into a strong, familiar hug.

He looked down into her face. "I'm so happy to see you, you have no idea."

"It's been so long, Nick. How are you? How did we get here, in Mexico? Can you believe this? I think it's crazy! I have so many questions for you. I just can't believe you're here. I haven't seen you since my wedding, it's been forever." Lucy knew she was rambling but she couldn't help herself. He was intimately close to her and she needed to fill the space between them with words.

Nicholas started to laugh. "Is it okay if I say something?"

159

Lucy stepped back shyly. "Sorry Nick, I talk fast when I'm nervous. I can't help myself."

"Don't be nervous, we can handle this."

Lucy looked up at him, her face softening and her heart relieved that this first encounter was finally over.

"God, I'm so happy to see you, Nick."

"Me too, Lucy, me too."

She stared at him for longer than she should have.

Alex and Carlos returned to the room with several other rifles and assault weapons. Things got serious again as Nick's face hardened into the intimidating expression she was used to. It was time to get back to work. She turned her attention back to Carlos, who was already setting up rifles and small handguns for her to try out. She glanced back at Nick, who had his eyes focused on her.

Carlos handed her a small .22-caliber rifle.

"*Gracias*, Carlos," she stated. She raised her weapon and let go of all her stress, anxiety, and nervousness as she fired off a powerful shot, her feet still and planted. She felt invigorated, strong, and sure of herself for the first time since she arrived in Mexico.

She smiled.

# CHAPTER 25

## *Charles*

Charles took Anna by the hand and lifted her up against his chest. Kat pushed Sammy in the stroller back toward Lucy and Jack's farmhouse. Anna appeared to be unaffected by Kat and Jack's confrontation and laid her head on Charles' shoulder, content in being carried and perhaps a little tired from their walk.

Charles glanced over at Kat. He could tell she was deeply upset, in thought over Jack. "Kat, you okay?" Charles stopped walking and took hold of Kat's hand.

Kat turned toward him and began to cry suddenly, burying her face into his arm so that Anna would not see her upset. Charles took a deep breath and let her cry, remaining silent as she did so, but turning Anna's head in the opposite direction.

Kat wiped her face and tears on Charles' T-shirt and turned away from him. "What if Jack's right, Charles? What if something horrible happens to Lucy? I'll never forgive myself. These poor children...I can hardly think about that."

Charles began walking again, wrapping his free arm around Kat as they moved up the road.

"Lucy's a smart and an intelligent woman, and you know Nicholas cares deeply for her. He would never let anything happen to her. I have a strong sense of security when it comes to Nick. I trust him to protect her. Don't you? In fact, I think Jack does too. He's just overwhelmed right now—and jealous."

"I feel so guilty. I'll be so relieved when everything's back to normal," Kat stated.

"There's no more normal for us here. It's been tragedy after tragedy." Charles looked down at the road as he thought about their situation. "Kat? What do you think about us settling down here, staying for some time? I feel like I need to help my brother get through this, to help him with the farm."

Charles looked over at Kat to see the slow smile start to spread quietly across her face.

"Really, Charles? Really, you'd like to stay? What about the commercial fishing? What about the boat?"

"We'll sell the boat. It's not important. I can always get another boat if we decide to go back east. But we have a real opportunity here, Kat. This farm is a *real* moneymaker, a consistent source of income that we could rely on. Perhaps we could start our own family and build our own house on Pop's land. I am his grandson as well. I deserve some of the benefits that should have been bestowed on my mother, God rest her soul, regardless of what Jack says."

Charles watched Kat take in this information. He was hoping that the words *family*, *children*, *home* would motivate her and gain her support for moving permanently to the farm.

Kat walk a steadier pace, seeming to be given a new sense of energy, her attitude suddenly changed and upbeat.

"Charles, perhaps we should think about getting married before we start a family."

Charles laughed under his breath; she was such a typical woman.

"Sure Kat, whatever you want."

Charles bent down and kissed Kat on her forehead. He was pleased with himself. All the bills, all the repairs on the boat, the financial strain…it could all end for him now. The drug addiction, he could handle. Now if everyone could just move on over this Pop thing, they could all go back to living again.

Charles smiled deviously. It was settled. He wasn't going anywhere.

# CHAPTER 26

*Anthony*

Anthony shoved a water bottle and a few snacks into his backpack, grabbed Jase, and threw him over his shoulder.

"Come on son, you'll be late for the soccer game."

Jase cried with excitement as he squirmed out of his father's arms to grab his soccer ball. He followed his father outside and into the car, talking animatedly about the upcoming game and about the play date he and his friend were having afterward.

"I'm going to run straight this time, right Dad? Straight for the goal."

"That's right son, no going backward, just forward."

Anthony smiled as he buckled his son into his booster seat and closed the vehicle door. When he got into the driver's side seat, he looked back into his rear view mirror at his son's face, thankful for the opportunity to share these special moments with him again.

Moments he thought he would never get back, moments that meant everything to him now.

"Are you ready, buddy? How many goals are you going to make today?" Anthony chuckled.

"A lot, Dad, a lot!"

"That's my boy."

Anthony pulled out of his driveway, and when he looked both ways for traffic, something struck him as odd. A car was pulled over on the side of the road, a few houses down from his. One man sat inside, casually smoking a cigarette, while the other looked dark and blurry because of the way the sun shone down upon the vehicle. Instantly, Anthony's heart raced. He wasn't sure but he felt like he was being watched, like those men were there for him. He had this feeling before, and although he was doing well at his job and he and Rose were adjusting to their life together again, he never wanted to let his guard down. He was paranoid about being alert. He paused and stared at the vehicle before pulling out of his driveway.

The vehicle followed him.

He drove recklessly through town, one eye on the road, one eye on the vehicle behind him. He pulled into the school parking lot and parked his car near the soccer field. Many cars lined the area and children were running everywhere. Saturday morning soccer was popular in their small town and Anthony was eager to disappear among the crowd with his son.

He couldn't live this way, in fear for his family. He wouldn't live this way.

Getting out of the vehicle, Anthony moved to go to the trunk. After tossing a few lawn chairs and other sports equipment out of his way, he lifted the compartment that held his spare tire and pulled out an automatic weapon, loaded it, and shoved it in his pants.

He then retrieved his son from the back seat and walked with him, hand-in-hand, to the field. He wanted to take Jase back home, to a place where he would be safe. Instead he opted to put him on the field, where he wouldn't be noticed among the other hundred children running around in soccer shorts and shin guards. Sweat dewed on Anthony's top lip and he wiped it away with the bottom of his T-shirt. He looked back at the parking lot—no sign of the vehicle that was following him. Maybe it was just his imagination.

He reached his son's teammates and watched Jase run out onto the soccer field, yelling with excitement as he grabbed a ball and kicked it around with his friends. Anthony stood on the sideline, deep in thought and contemplation. He watched his son and it reminded him of a time when he and his best friend Nicholas would play baseball together, when he lived in Boston so many years ago. Did Nicholas know he had been released from prison? Anthony wished that he could convey to him how sorry he was, how he knew that he had disappointed him over and over again. *I've changed*, he wanted to tell Nick. *My friendship with you was the only true friendship I had ever known my entire life.*

Anthony took a deep breath. His anxiety and paranoia was starting to fade. Then his phone rang. He glanced down at the handheld device.

A familiar number appeared, one he could never forget.

*Garcia.*

Anthony knew then that his past was never going to leave him. Being released from prison didn't release him from the history that he had created, and deep down, he understood that.

He would handle the situation and leave town with his family. It needed to be done, and it needed to be smart.

He was better than everybody now.

# CHAPTER 27

*Lucy*

Nicholas dropped Lucy off at her hotel room. She was confident that she had helped him, to prepare him for what would come tonight, if her intuition were correct.

Lucy got the sense that Anthony was nervous. He went out of his way to avoid things, certain places and people. His energy was edgy and jumpy, as if he were waiting for something bad to happen. Anthony's wife, however…she was a very confident woman. Intuitive in her own way, she had been protecting and defending Anthony for years. She was a family warrior, a caretaker, a mother and a lover. The snapshots of her were stunning; she was a natural beauty and a very attentive mother to her son.

Lucy felt sorry for her. She could feel Rose's energy, the worry she held that something bad could happen to her family and that she would lose Anthony again. Lucy could almost hear the prayers that Rose would repeat every night for her family, prayers of safety and protection. It was an awful feeling, knowing that Nicholas was investigating him, watching him. Lucy was aiding Nick, and although she had agreed to help him, she couldn't help but connect and feel sorry for Anthony's family as well. It was like Anthony was just trying to figure it out too, but for some reason, Nicholas had it in for him. Lucy sensed that Anthony may be an innocent bystander, a victim that needed to be sacrificed for the greater good of all those involved.

Lucy stood in the middle of her hotel room. Nicholas had offered to walk her up, but she felt strong and didn't want to rely on him to accompany her everywhere she went. She had agreed, however, to have dinner with him that night and she hoped that maybe through dinner, he would begin to open up to her. She wished she had something nice to wear; she felt that this would be a special dinner between the two of them. She hated to feel excited about it, but it had been awhile since anyone had taken her out without her children. It felt nice.

Thoughts of Jack entered her brain. She couldn't help but feel angry toward him. After years of having tolerated his controlling ways and the unexplained resentment he had for her, it felt wonderful to be away from him. She loved Jack, she wanted to help him, but he had to want it too. Maybe he would realize, while she was gone, that he had been tough on her. Maybe he would be sorry and things could change between them.

She was enamored with the tropical feel of the town she was in, its palm trees, the mountains and the waterfront. The town of Chapala was as lovely and idealistic as any romance novel she had ever read. The brightly colored village with cobbled streets and vintage architecture was inspiring. The exotic traditions of the natives were different and new and Lucy loved every bit of the culture she had experienced so far. She wanted to see more of it, to experience some of the nightlife and to spend time with Nicholas, to talk and to catch up on personal things. So far the only conversations they'd had were about the criminal outfit they were hunting down and the proper way to load and unload numerous types of guns and weaponry.

She wanted to feel relaxed.

Picking up the phone, she dialed the front desk. She wasn't sure what she needed, but she hoped that maybe *la señora* could direct her to a clothing boutique so she could purchase something nice to wear for her dinner, something that wouldn't make her look so out of place.

The phone rang and rang but no one answered. Lucy hung up the phone and decided to go downstairs to see if she could find her.

Lucy made her way down the hallway, then down the small staircase that opened up into the main reception area. Señora was there, speaking with another couple seemingly on their honeymoon, for Señora kept repeating, "Congratulations, congratulations" in her best American accent. Lucy caught her eye and she smiled and held her finger up, as if to say she'd be with her in a moment.

Past the reception desk, Lucy glanced down at the travel brochures that lined the wall near the sitting area. She picked up one brochure for hand gliding, one for a fishing boat extravaganza, and another for a rainforest zip lining company. *I wish I had some time to do a little exploring while I'm here,* she thought. But she needed to return home as soon as possible.

"*Hola*! How are you, Miss Lucy?" Señora came bounding toward Lucy, and Lucy couldn't help but feel the warmth and affection from this woman. She was so sweet and loving toward her, the way she hugged her and pulled her hair up off her face and behind her shoulders. Lucy loved the attention; it reminded her of her own mother, whom she missed dearly. She'd been so busy with her own family and her own children that she forgot how it felt to have someone care for you, like a mother. She missed it.

"How can I help you?" Señora asked as she looked up into Lucy's face. Señora was a good one-foot shorter than Lucy, her short stature and plump figure making her even more matronly.

"Señora?" Lucy asked. "I was wondering if you could tell me where I may find a dress boutique, some place where I can buy something to wear to dinner…not too fancy, but not too casual either." Lucy looked into the hotel owner's eyes.

Señora beamed up at Lucy, excitement exuding from her smile.

"I have a dinner date tonight, and I have not brought proper clothing."

"*Si, si,* come with me," Señora said as she pulled Lucy from the reception area, around the corner to a back door. Señora knocked on the door several times and waited for it to open. Lucy stood and listened to footsteps approach from behind the door. Locks and bolts clicked and then the doorknob finally turned, allowing the ladies to walk through into a storage room riddled with boxes, clothing, mannequins, and other various types of retail paraphernalia. The woman behind the door was dressed professionally in a white tailored suit, white sling-back heels and her hair was neatly coiled around the top of her head. Her tanned skin appeared golden against the bright white she wore. She was elegant and beautiful and just as warm and welcoming as Señora.

"Miss Lucy, this is my sister, Giselle," Señora said. "This is her boutique; she will take very good care of you and help you find what you need." Señora leaned over and half hugged her sister while they exchanged a rapid display of words, none of which Lucy could understand, but she didn't care. She loved to hear their native tongue. Señora said goodbye and then Giselle took Lucy's hand and walked her through the back storage area, which opened up to the most beautiful clothing boutique Lucy had ever seen.

The floors were tiled with white marble and the ceilings were high with a large chandelier hanging between two rotating fans. Retail shelves lined the walls on either side with neatly folded articles of clothing. Four beautiful white leather couches formed a perfect square below the chandelier. It was lovely. Lucy followed Giselle around the room while she offered her several appropriate garments along with inappropriate outfits. Although Lucy would never consider wearing some of the things that were presented to her, she also realized that the Mexican women were far more daring in their ensembles than she had ever been. Perhaps she should try to fit in just a little, embrace the culture with style and wear something she may never be able to wear again.

"Giselle, do you have something a little bit more simple…sexy but simple?" Lucy asked quietly, not wanting any of the other patrons to hear her. Giselle smiled and looked Lucy up and down. She lifted Lucy's arms to her side and seemed to focus her stare mainly on Lucy's breasts. Lucy felt her cheeks flame.

"Come, come with me, Miss Lucy."

Lucy followed Giselle into a private dressing room and stood in the middle, glancing into the mirrors all around her, hating her hair, hating her figure and her outfit she had been in all day long. Lucy sighed and slumped down into a chair along the wall.

"You stay here, I'll be right back," Giselle said.

Lucy thought about her family back home. She needed to speak to Jack as soon as she got back to the room. Kat had made it very clear that Jack was very upset with her earlier on the phone. She dreaded making the phone call; it was giving her anxiety. She might even postpone it another day. What difference did it make? There was nothing he could do now; she wasn't about to jump on a plane and go home.

Giselle came back into the room with several simple dresses and hung them on the wall. She also brought some undergarments, sexy in nature but appropriate for the dresses. Lucy stared at Giselle and waited for her to leave the room. Giselle just stood there, staring back at her, looking at her as if to say, "Well? Get on with it. Try something on."

Lucy turned around and looked at herself again in the mirror. She began to undress herself, removing her cowgirl boots, slipping her jeans off over her hips, and pulling her simple but pretty top over her head. She stood and stared at herself. She was *still* wearing a nursing bra. *Oh god*, she thought, *what a mess I am*. Lucy turned and faced Giselle who looked upon her with loving, maternal eyes. "You are beautiful, Miss Lucy. Beautiful. No reason to look disappointed in yourself, Miss. Giselle is here to help you look as perfect as you are."

"You're very kind, Giselle. I don't know what has happened to me. I feel so awful about myself."

Giselle removed a pink satin bra and its matching bikini underwear from its hanger and handed it to Lucy. Had Lucy been with anyone else, she would have been horrified, but Giselle seemed not to care about nudity or anyone else's privacy. Lucy chuckled to herself; she could hardly bring herself to undress except that Giselle had halfway started to unhook Lucy's bra while Lucy was contemplating her shyness. Giselle turned Lucy around again to face the mirror and helped her try on the perfectly fitted, gloriously beautiful undergarment that made her feel like a woman.

Giselle smiled proudly while she readjusted Lucy's boobs, lifting them up just so that the soft cleavage could be seen. Lucy could not help but grin. What a difference a real bra made.

"Giselle! I love it! It's beautiful, I can't believe these are my boobs!"

Giselle laughed out loud. "I told you, you are beautiful! Now here, try on this dress." Giselle removed a scarlet-colored dress from a hanger. "You've had babies, Miss Lucy. You are busy, but you always must remember to take good care of yourself."

Lucy smiled deeply. The women she met on this trip had been the most wonderful people. She couldn't help but to take in all of their attention, and was enjoying very much their affection. Lucy slipped on the dress. Silk in material, the fabric floated around Lucy's body, landing on every curve of her figure. Every inch of softness was accentuated, the brightly colored material flowing lightly over her breast and then scooping down along the neckline, allowing for some cleavage to show, but conservative enough to make Lucy feel comfortable. The dress was perfect!

Giselle spun Lucy around and around, pleased with her selection. She handed Lucy a silver, open-toed heel with one delicate strap that circled her ankle. It was the perfect combination.

"Miss Giselle, thank you so much," Lucy gushed. "I appreciate your help and encouragement."

"I want you to enjoy tonight and stun your date into submission," Giselle said teasingly.

Lucy's eyes went wide. Did she want to do that? Was this too much? Oh my god, Nicholas would think that she's crazy. Giselle smiled mischievously and told Lucy she would meet her at the checkout counter. Lucy dressed and walked out of the changing room, deep in concentration.

Her face was suddenly in a frown of concern as Giselle wrapped up her purchases.

Giselle lifted Lucy's chin and looked her straight in the eyes.

"Your mother is so proud of you, and you should be too. Don't worry so much about your date, because life is short. Live and enjoy the moments as they come, okay Miss Lucy?"

Lucy nodded and began to digest the words. She reached over the counter and kissed Giselle twice, once on each cheek, and held her hands tight.

"Thank you, Giselle. Thank you so much."

"Goodbye, Lucy."

# CHAPTER 28

## *Jack*

Jack stood on Pop's porch and waited for Susie Mae to return. He paced the porch, back and forth, sitting still in the chair for a moment and then back up again, striding from one end of the porch to the other. He was full of so much angst, he needed to speak to someone he trusted...and that someone was Susie Mae. He settled back into the chair and took his hat off, running his fingers through his thick, sweaty hair, and then placed the hat back on his head.

There had to be something that they were missing. Something about Pop's death didn't make sense. Jack rose from the rocking chair and walked through the porch screen door, entering the small farmhouse kitchen. He stood in the cozy room and looked around. The countertops were tidy and neat. The table was cleared and free of Pop's newspapers and the agricultural magazines that he loved to leave around. The smell of baking was gone now but they were still there, part of some distant memory. The experiences he'd grown up with, coming home from school or from working in the fields, sitting with Pop and Susie Mae as they enjoyed a meal together. He felt a true sense of family when he was with them, the feeling that he was loved, a security that he had never known from his own family, his mother and his brother. Things had changed and Jack wanted to have it all back again.

He walked over to the refrigerator and opened the door. He grabbed a beer, cracked it open, and drank it. Cold and refreshing, it immediately relaxed him. He finished the beer, took another one, and headed outside to wait for Susie Mae.

He sat on the front steps of the porch, looking out toward the barn where Pop's body was discovered. He remembered lifting Pop's stiff and cold body off the barn floor, his clothing drenched in blood. He carried him to the ambulance that awaited, Susie Mae crying by his side. There was nothing they could do. They were too late; Pop was gone. The images of Pop's dead body still haunted him. He felt like a failure.

Wind blew and dust spiraled in front of it, creating a funnel cloud of dancing leaves and dried debris. Jack avoided the barn as often as he could, but today, he seemed drawn to it. He walked deliberately down the stone driveway, determined in his cause that there was something they had missed. Something just didn't make sense.

He recklessly took the last swig of his beer bottle and tossed the glass alongside the fence that bordered the driveway. The beer bottle rolled several times before clinking to a stop against a large potted planter. Jack grabbed hold of the barn access handle and slid the heavy door to the side, revealing an opening large enough to unload the horses or to drive farm equipment into the building. Jack walked up the ramp, pausing at the top and staring into the dark space within. The building had been emptied and deserted, all the horses moved into another barn closer to Jack's home, so he and Lucy could care for them. The emptiness inside echoed up through the rafters as dust and particles danced through the somber air.

Jack thought about how many times he had entered this barn. When he was young, Pop would follow him while Jack did his chores, and with his arms crossed, he would watch Jack and point. "Clean this! Move that over there!" Jack would move to his demands, eager to please him and make him proud. Pop always hounded him about keeping everything in good order. But it was good for Jack. It was what he needed—responsibility.

Jack's chest felt tight as he took a deep breath. The anxiety he felt was unmanageable at times. He missed him; he missed his demands and expectations. Everything Pop did was for Jack's benefit. He was hard on Jack, but he loved Jack unconditionally.

Jack thought about Susie Mae. She still tended to the smaller farm animals, the chickens and goats. Susie Mae was strong, but she was getting older, her spirit had been diminished and her sorrow noticeably affected her drive to work in her older years. Jack didn't want to take everything away from her because that would be heartbreaking, but he also didn't want to overburden her with the stress of maintaining the farm as well.

It was his responsibility now—Pop made that clear. Susie Mae was to be taken care of until she died, and Jack had no intention of having it any other way. It was difficult to imagine that someday Susie would be gone too, and all he would have left were the memories of his family and how they had once lived. It was hard to envision the farm without Pop and Susie, but yet, here Jack was, alone again, making hard decisions and hoping for the best. He had always loved the farm; he loved the hard work and the satisfaction he received. He imagined that someday, his son Sammy would also follow in his footsteps and that he would have the same companionship with his boy that he and his grandfather shared. Someday he would leave Sammy with the legacy and honorable reputation of the farm.

Jack stepped into the barn, his cowboy boots loud and echoing in the empty space. He walked past the horse stalls, and paused. He recalled the moment he and Lucy had their first official kiss. He took a deep breath. He closed his eyes and prayed, prayed for her safety and for the Lord to bring her home to him again. It seemed unreasonable to him that he may lose his wife, after all they'd been through, but nevertheless he felt it. He had been failing at his marriage for years now, he knew. It was his pride that hurt him; the *voice* that convinced him Lucy was strong enough to endure his behaviors and that she didn't need Jack in many ways. He didn't want to appear weak to her, so he ignored her, keeping her at a safe emotional distance.

In that barn, he made a decision.

He was going to change.

He needed to be strong for his family and his wife, maybe even vulnerable. He considered following her to Mexico, to fight for her. He was afraid of what he would find; he was afraid to know the truth, good or bad.

Around the corner where they stored the hay bales was where Pop's body was found. Standing in the middle of the room, Jack felt the overwhelming pain and torture of the loss surface through his grieving chest. He envisioned his grandfather struggling with his killer, fighting back as best as his elderly body could.

Jack fell down to his knees and looked up toward the rafters. A sob escaped him. He spoke to his grandfather in tones of torture and confusion, pleading with him to send him a sign, to tell him who had done this to them.

"Please Pop, please help me," he wailed.

A hand touched his shoulder. Susie Mae moved toward him, sitting on the floor next to him and holding him while he wept. Jack buried his face in her apron and sobbed tears that he had held in so deeply, tears of failure and the overwhelming torture that he felt, grasping at her. Susie Mae rocked him quietly as she did so many years before, when Jack was just a young boy, after his mother died. She soothed him and stroked his hair and spoke quietly to him. "Let it all out my boy, it's okay. Let it all out."

They held each other.

He needed her to love him. She was the only mother he had ever known and the only person who could help him now.

She was all he had left.

# CHAPTER 29

## *Jack*

Jack walked back up to Pop's farmhouse, Susie Mae at his side, holding on to his arm like she would any other time. Jack felt drained, but better. He had been suffering for too long and it was time that he move forward positively instead of lingering in this awful place of self-torture. He knew he had an obsession to find Pop's murderer, but he needed to let go some of his guilt. He blamed himself for not being there when Pop needed him. He felt somehow solely responsible for Pop's death and that to absolve himself, he needed to find Pop's murderer and finish what they had started. It was consuming him and ruining his family—he could see that clearly now.

Jack opened the screen door for Susie Mae and watched her move across the kitchen floor straight for the teapot. Jack excused himself and walked into the bathroom. He looked at himself in the mirror and turned on the frigid cold water. He let the water collect in the small sink basin, then splashed his face roughly, rubbing his

185

skin and his eyes, letting the cold water drip off him. Again he splashed his face, reaching for a towel on the countertop, its edges lined with a pretty lace design. He figured this towel was meant to be for decoration only but he grabbed it anyway. He felt exhausted. He wanted to see his children. He wanted Lucy.

Jack walked back into the kitchen and sat down at the table where Susie had placed his cup of tea and a nice arrangement of cookies and pie. Jack smiled and glanced up at her while she bent down and kissed him on his cheek.

"You always knew how to make me feel better, Susie."

Susie Mae snickered and leaned up against the counter with her arms crossed. Jack stared down at his teacup and played with the cookies that she had left him, not quite sure if he was going to eat one or not.

"Do you remember when you were young and you told poor little Angie that you were going to walk back home to Connecticut?"

Jack chuckled.

"You had that old map that you found buried in one of Pop's old dressers."

Jack smiled. "Poor Angie. I don't think she ever forgave me for that. She ran home to you crying, begging for you to go find me."

Susie Mae walked over to Jack, pulled out a chair for herself, and grabbed his hand.

"You had a real hard time when you moved here, Jack. I worried for you for a long time, but you came around. You came around and you completed our family."

Jack could feel his chest restrict. He closed his eyes and looked down at the table; taking deep breaths, he fought back the urge to cry. They were both still so emotionally damaged.

"Pop had always spoken about your mother and the guilt he felt about the loss of her and you boys. When you came back into Pop's life, it was like he was a different man. He had a joy in his eyes that I had never seen, a pride and a sense of hope again. You were everything to him as I know he was everything to you."

Jack sat and listened to Susie's words, words that he knew were spoken truths. Jack and his Pop had a special bond between them and it only grew stronger as the years passed.

"Pop would be disappointed now if he knew that you were failing the things that you both cared for so deeply." Susie Mae looked at him, and Jack felt as if she were peering into his soul. "I know you feel lost, Jack, but it's time now to stand up and be that little boy who came around. I know you have it in you. You're a younger version of Pop, and you have the strength and courage to move forward and to work hard. Your family needs you—your children, your wife—and this farm and I need you. You are the patriarch now, and you need to start to respect that role and do right by us all."

Jack had a great respect for Susie Mae; he knew the words she spoke were genuine and loving.

"I'm sorry, Susie Mae," he murmured. "I'm sorry for acting such a fool." Jack held on to Susie Mae by both her hands and stared into her eyes. "I promise you, I won't let you down. I promise you, I will be the man that I'm expected to be and to take care of this family. It's just been…"

"It's been hard, I understand." Susie Mae placed her tired hand on Jack's face. "We have many challenges that we still face and we need to work together as a family to get through it all. It's time now to put down the alcohol, and to ask for the strength we will need to move forward again and to heal."

Susie Mae stood from the table and pulled Jack into a strong embrace. Jack's height towered over hers but she held him firm, as if she thought that the harder she squeezed him, the more love he would feel from her.

"I love you, Jack. I know you will do the right things."

"I love you too, Susie Mae." Jack gathered his hat and moved toward the front screen door.

"Where are you going, Jack?" she asked.

"I'm going to see my children."

# CHAPTER 30

## *Lucy*

Lucy walked out of the boutique satisfied with her purchases and acutely aware that her intentions with Nicholas were deceptive. She couldn't help but feel that she needed to finish something that they had started a long time ago. Perhaps then, she would be able to move on with Jack, holding no regret for the past and confirming that she was meant to be with him.

That's what she told herself, anyway.

The truth was, Lucy didn't understand why she felt the way she did toward Nicholas. He pulled on her spirit and unexplainably she thought she might have loved him. Not knowing the truth, putting her trust in her instincts as they pushed her forward, she was convinced that things didn't happen accidentally or without purpose. She needed to understand her purpose and so she reasoned with the voice, convinced that this was the right thing to do.

She walked leisurely, looking around the surrounding area. She noticed a farmer's market at the corner and she wanted to grab a few things before going back to her room.

She walked down the street with her bags in her hand, listening to the patrons as she approached the crowded area. She would never tire of hearing affluent Spanish and she wished she had learned a second language. The words made her feel sexy, unique and foreign, like she could pretend to be someone she wasn't. She wasn't a wife and a mother, but a stranger in a strange land, absorbing all the wonderful things that the foreign town had to offer her...and she loved it.

She strolled down the aisles of handmade crafts, items of fabric, hats, purses, and jewelry. She walked up and down the aisles of fruits and vegetables, witnessing vendors selling everything from the commonly known orange to the exotic-looking pitahaya. Lucy grabbed fruit she had never tried before, and filled her basket with flowers and strange-looking vegetables. She found an adorable hat for Anna and a small toy for Sammy. Although she missed her children, she knew that they were safe and well cared for. She welcomed the break from the monotony and the stress of her daily life.

Lucy wandered a little farther and came across an antique shop full of furniture and old household items. She climbed the few steps to the entrance, about to open the door when a woman walked out of the store and passed her on the stairway. She turned and watched the woman as she left, and was surprised that she recognized her. The photos and pictures she had reviewed with Alex and the boys were still fresh in her mind. The woman was Rose, Anthony's wife. Lucy was startled at first as she watched her pass but then she turned, following her down the stairs and through the crowd. Rose's black hair was tied neatly behind her head and she wore a sun hat. She moved so effortlessly, her body wrapped in a fitted sundress; she walked through the crowd as people moved out of her way. She was breathtaking.

Lucy followed her past the farmer's market toward the marina. As the crowd started to dissipate, Lucy lingered farther back, so Rose wouldn't notice her. She wished she wasn't so boggled down with all the bags, but she was so interested in Rose and where she was heading that she continued forward. Perhaps she would find out something about her that would be helpful to Nicholas.

Rose stopped to say hello to a familiar face and Lucy swore that Rose had turned and caught her eye. Lucy stopped walking and dropped one of her bags, hoping to create a distraction. She fumbled with her purchases and then waited for Rose to be on the move again. Rose continued walking and seemed to have no interest in Lucy.

192

Rose disappeared between two large brick buildings. The area was becoming less and less populated; Lucy wondered if this was where Rose lived with her family. *Should I continue following her?*

"I've gone this far," she mumbled, and she shrugged her shoulders.

Lucy rounded the corner of the building and stopped, surprised by Rose, who stood waiting for her.

Lucy dropped all of her belongings. The shock of horror and embarrassment spread across her face as her hands shook; she was startled and a little scared.

"*¿Qué quieres?*" Rose demanded as she pointed directly into Lucy's face, a small shimmer gleaming from her eye as she stood up to Lucy. Lucy didn't know what she said and gave a little shake of her head. Rose paused. "What do you want?"

Lucy thought she might die. She had never been confrontational. She needed to explain this, but didn't know how. She reached down and all around her, gathering up her belongings and stumbling over her speech as she did so. "I'm sorry ma'am, I didn't mean to upset you." *Think, Lucy, think!* "It's just that you are stunning and I love your sundress. As you can see, I love to shop." Lucy held up her packages and purchases, just to prove her point. "I was hoping you would allow me to take a picture, so that I may search for the dress…perhaps you bought it locally?" Lucy hoped her voice didn't sound as nervous as her stomach felt.

Rose looked Lucy up and down from her shoes to her clothes and then went on to inspect Lucy's hair, judging her appearance as if she were a child on the way to Sunday mass. Lucy smiled, hoping to appear relaxed and easygoing.

Rose suddenly laughed, throwing her hands up as she grabbed ahold of Lucy's arm. "Oh, of course! You are so kind." Rose looked down at her own dress and smoothed out the material with her hands, granting Lucy the view of her curves. "Thank you for your lovely compliment. Come, come with me, we will have coffee and I will tell you where I shop!" She pulled Lucy down the brick street, through the aroma of the open coffee shops and the bakery on the corner. Lucy was completely stunned at Rose's openhearted friendliness; she was genuine in nature and sincere in her invitation. Lucy longed to sit with her, to find out everything she could about her.

"No, no, no, I couldn't inconvenience you that way. I have somewhere to be." Lucy would have adored sitting and having coffee with Rose, but she knew that it would be wrong and deceitful. Lucy's intentions were misleading and although she was in Mexico on a mission, Lucy wasn't calculating and dishonest by nature.

Lucy stepped backward, back toward the street she had just come from, back toward the farmer's market, where she would mix in with the crowd and slither back into her hotel room where she could breathe again.

"Wait, wait," Rose yelled as Lucy scurried away.

"Thank you, sorry to bother you. Take care now." Lucy waved. She continued walking, turning her back on Rose and hurriedly making her way up the street.

# CHAPTER 31

*Nicholas*

After Nicholas dropped Lucy off at her hotel, he went to the marina, where he and Alex were staying. He was distracted by his thoughts, overwhelmingly concerned for what lay ahead of him and his group of vigilantes. He wanted Anthony to answer some questions, but not as much as he wanted this fight to be over with. Why would Anthony come back to this place to settle down in a location that held so many temptations for him?

It was a beautiful city, Chapala, full of history and architecture. If Nick were here on vacation, he would have taken long walks on the sandy beach and explored the mountain range with his children. He wanted nothing more than to enjoy his kids and to live his life without the fear of revenge lingering over his head. He thought about his career, how successful and proud he was of the life he had made. It was all at risk now—his job, his family, and the safety of his children. There was no going back; it was now or never and he prayed that he had the strength and power to battle.

Nick parked his car discreetly on the side of the road and looked around the street before he exited his vehicle. He entered the back alleyway behind his hotel and climbed the fire escape, entering the building through the third floor balcony. He opened the door and walked down the floral-patterned hotel hallway and entered his room, undetected. The front lobby entrance of the hotel had been under construction and for many other reasons, Nick preferred to remain unrecognized for as long as possible.

His plan was to assassinate Garcia and possibly Anthony if need be, then leave Chapala, as if he were never there. It was possibly the most terrifying feeling to plot and plan the murder of another human being. As a police officer, it was something he had always fought against. He had killed before, but it had been in the line of duty and in self-defense. He was not a murderer. He captured murderers and put them in jail—that was his job. Nicholas knew that Garcia had been following Anthony. He also knew that Anthony's life was in danger and that Garcia was not going to let Anthony survive after he had testified against him in court. It was so foolish for Anthony to come back to Mexico. His family wasn't safe here; he should have settled somewhere else.

Nick sighed. He wanted to shave, but he felt tired. He wanted to nap, but there was no time. He wanted to tell Lucy she looked beautiful, but he couldn't. When he thought about Lucy, his mind stayed there. It was complicated with Lucy; she was exactly

197

how he remembered her, but far more confident and mature than she had ever been. She was unafraid, yet she looked at him for direction. She was brave, but she needed him to feel brave. It was a great responsibility, and he took it very seriously. He wanted to trust her, but he didn't want to scare her any more than need be.

Nicholas' phone ring. His wife's name appeared on the caller ID. He closed his eyes; he knew that she would be in a panic. He had avoided this conversation with her, dreading her words. Nick took a deep breath and answered her call.

"Hey honey, how are you?"

He could hear that Beth was crying.

"What the fuck is going on? I've got two kids here tired and cranky and this is what I come home to? A handwritten note, are you kidding me?"

"Beth honey, calm down." Nicholas rolled his eyes and stood to pace the hotel room.

"Nicholas, why didn't you tell me you were leaving? I deserve to know these things." She paused and took a deep breath, her voice cracking with emotion. "Nick, where are you?"

"I'm in Mexico." Nick waited, flinching as he heard the words coming out of his own mouth. He knew he should be with his family, but he needed to protect them, he needed to end this. Silence filtered through the phone. "Beth? Are you still there?"

"I'm taking the kids to my mother's." Beth sobbed over the phone line. "I don't understand you, Nick," she cried. "I feel alone in this family, I don't know where you are, I don't know where you've been…it's like you're a figment of my imagination floating in and out of our lives, whenever it suits you. I can't live this way anymore. You don't love me, it's clear."

Nick heard his wife's words and his stomach turned. She didn't understand, and no words that he could say would make her understand.

"I'm sorry, Beth. I have to do the right thing now, even though it doesn't feel like the right thing. Please, kiss the children for me; tell them that I love them. I love you, Beth."

"Goodbye, Nick." The phone clicked. Silence.

Nicholas sat, staring at the receiver. Letting out a deep sigh of frustration, he vowed that he would make it up to her. He prayed she would wait for him.

Alex walked into the room, his face determined as he threw the local newspaper down on Nick's lap. *Un Festival en la Ciudad* was headlined in bold with bright pictures of local merchants and citizens dressed in costume.

"Tonight," Alex said with confidence.

Nicholas nodded his head at his partner.

"Tonight."

# CHAPTER 32

## *Charles*

Charles hid behind the barn and waited for Susie Mae to leave for church. She was taking her sweet time and he was beginning to get irritated with her. He didn't have much time to waste. Jack would be leaving his house soon to work around the farm, and Charles wasn't sure where he would be and when.

Charles took a drag off his cigarette and then stomped it out in the dirt. He looked at his watch and back up at the farmhouse. "Come on, old bag," he muttered.

Susie Mae gingerly exited the house and shut the screen door behind her. She walked down the few steps off the porch and headed toward her car in her Sunday best. Charles was at full attention, waiting for her to start the engine and eyeing her as she left the farm driveway. Once she was completely out of sight, he made his way to the farmhouse, his eyes darting; he opened the front door and walked in, shutting the door behind him.

His long legs carried him through the kitchen as he made his way into the bathroom off his grandfather's bedroom. He opened the medicine cabinet, and reaching in, he grabbed every medicine container and read their labels.

"Lisinopril? What the fuck is that? Synthroid...Tylenol...Penicillin! These aren't shit..." Charles spoke to himself. "Wait a minute, wait a minute...Tylenol with Codeine! Nice!" Charles shoved the bottle of pills in his back pocket.

He entered his grandfather's parlor, going straight to his work desk, opening the drawers and flipping through papers and folders, looking for something, but of what he wasn't sure. He wanted the deed, he knew. He wanted to know who the farm was left to, and if he was entitled to any of his grandfather's estate. Susie Mae and Jack were named as executors in Pop's will, but they were very private about the finances of the farm and the distribution of his assets. Susie Mae tried to put Charles at ease by mentioning that Pop did not forget about him, that he was going to receive some sort of inheritance. Jack, however, was eager to share the fact that Charles shouldn't be expecting much. Pop and Charles, they didn't have the closest of relationships, they never spent time together, but Charles wanted to see for himself. He believed he was owed at least a third of the estate; he was a blood relative and that ought to mean something.

Charles continued to look, slamming the drawers in frustration at the lack of information. He moved into Pop's bedroom. He looked under the bed, in the closets and in boxes of personal items that Susie Mae had been packing.

He needed money. His drug habit was costly. He dreaded coming to the farm, but now with the unfortunate (or fortunate) event of Pop's death, it may mean the chance to breathe easy and to stay on at the farm permanently, his family naïve to his motives.

Charles paused at the doorway, running his hands carelessly through his hair. "What the fuck!" he screamed as he kicked the kitchen garbage can.

Charles looked one more time around the house for any kind of safe, any kind of hiding spot. Nothing.

He strode through the house, feeling the same agitation he had felt years before when he heard that Jack had spent his growing up years in a safe and warm place, with the love and affection of two adoring grandparents. Charles had suffered, living place to place, not knowing when he would eat and how he would survive. It wasn't fair; he wanted his share of the pie.

Charles stopped in the kitchen and glanced out the window. Jack was in the field, tinkering with one of the tractors. He narrowed his eyes in on his brother. How different they were, he mused, yet they were both the same: broken.

Charles left the farmhouse and slammed the door behind him. It was time to go to plan B. He wouldn't stop until he got what was rightfully his.

Fair was fair.

# CHAPTER 33

*Jack*

It was in their last meeting that things started to change for Jack.

Jack watched Charles intently as his brother made his regular speech, walking back and forth on the dirt floor of the small abandoned greenhouse.

"Those fucking Mexicans did this to us," he spat, pointing at the farmers. "You know it and I know it."

"But Charles, we need the laborers. You're not a farmer, you don't understand."

"Mr. Nelson," Charles stated calmly, "am I to believe that you would put your family at risk, your wives and your children, for the cost of cheap Mexican labor?"

The crowd started to argue among themselves. Jack rolled his eyes and leaned back in his chair, folding his arms over his

**205**

stomach. It was the same thing every week. Charles would make his speech and incite the farmers, and then turn to booze and alcohol and then gunshots and target practice.

Jack scanned the concerned faces of the local farmers, people—now friends—that he had come to know and care for. Their concern for Pop and for Jack was genuine and it was humbling, but these men had families and farms of their own.

He thought about something Lucy had said to him the day after pop's death. She had been crying, her face was wet with tears and her eyes swollen red. Kat and Charles had taken the children into town to give the tortured couple a chance to talk. Lucy had collapsed into Jack's chest, clinging onto his shirt with her hands.

"Jack, the visions, they're not clear. Pop was unafraid; he was relaxed when he died. I can feel his calmness and see his smile. But then the brutality—there was so much *anger*. It was as if Pop couldn't believe it, he wouldn't believe it. But it's so unclear, I can't think straight; the pain is too deep and my emotions are so unstable."

Jack held his wife, listening to her sob. People loved Pop, everyone did. The entire town came to his birthday party; the entire town came to his funeral. Pop wasn't robbed and nothing was stolen. Why was there anger in his death?

Jack was tired. His friends, the people who supported him; they were tired. It had been months now since Pop died, and they weren't any closer to finding his killer than they were on the first day.

Jack stood and approached Charles, placing his hand on his shoulder and nodding his head, indicating to him that he wanted to speak. Charles reluctantly stood aside and let Jack lead the meeting.

The group of men grew quiet. They all stared at Jack, waiting for him to continue.

Jack cleared his throat. "It's over, fellas. I'm done."

"What?" Mitt Johnson leaned over to Leroy McCain and whispered in his ear, "What did he just say?"

"Sorry Mitt, everybody. Your support has meant everything to me and I will never forget it. Pop's murderer is gone; he is no longer among us. I'm sure and I think it's just time for us to move on."

Charles stood up, and his chair scooted across the floor behind him. "What are you talking about, Jack? Do you know something we don't know?" Charles' voice roared over the low level of banter and complaints as he spoke on everyone's behalf in the room.

"It's over, Charles. I'm not doing this anymore."

"You know what, Jack, there's something wrong here. You can't just stand up here and tell us all to go home now. These men have farms; we're all at risk. We don't understand why you would want to quit now."

"I don't need to explain to you, Charles. If you can't understand, perhaps you haven't been paying attention. This has been a huge waste of time and I'm not doing this anymore. Now if you don't mind, I'm going to go home now, to my family."

Charles reached out and grabbed Jack by the arm, preventing him from turning away from him. Jack stopped short and turned back to Charles, his eyes narrowing in on him, his patience wearing thin. Jack's entire body stiffened; adrenaline pumped through his blood as he squeezed his fist tightly, not wanting to get into a physical altercation with his brother, but ready if he needed to be.

"I don't answer to you, Charles," he hissed. "You don't get a say in this. I suggest you take your hand off me and stay out of my way."

Charles released Jack and stepped back.

"Well, we don't have to stand back and do nothing, Jack. We can continue on our efforts to find Pop's killer, with or without you. We don't need you, Jack."

The group of men gathered around Charles and several men agreed with him.

Jack stared at the men in the room and took a deep breath. His fight wasn't with them.

"Good night, men."

Jack turned and left the building.

# CHAPTER 34

*Lucy*

Lucy walked down the stairs into the hotel lobby, stopping in the hallway mirror to glance at herself. She felt confident that Nicholas would notice her—hopeful, anyway—but her stomach felt uneasy. Perhaps she may have overdressed for their dinner. Her time with Nick would be short lived and she would be returning home soon to be with her own family. She was beginning to second-guess herself; maybe she was making a great mistake. She was taking a risk, but it was an appealing one, and she was starving for the excitement and the thrill that she felt years before with Nicholas, before she had been married and before she had her children.

She took a deep breath and smoothed her hands over her silky dress. "Nicholas will be impressed," she stated to the mirror as she ran her hand along the inside of her thigh, confirming that her small firearm was still in place and perfectly concealed. She grinned, thinking about Nick and how the obscured weapon would probably be his favorite part of her outfit, an accessory that would definitely please him the most.

Lucy continued down the stairs, eager to meet Señora in the parlor. The woman was there waiting, fluffing the pillows in the lounge area and neatly rearranging the magazine and newspapers back in their proper places. Señora stopped what she was doing and stood straight, eyeing Lucy thoroughly, taking in her pretty heels and shapely body. She examined her up and down, and then settled her stare, looking into her eyes.

"Ah, Miss Lucy, come to me. Come, let me take a look at you." Señora waved Lucy toward her and reached for her hands as she pulled her into a motherly embrace. "My sister, she outdid herself. You are stunning, Miss Lucy. Oh, your face." Señora squeezed Lucy's cheeks. "How do you feel, do you like?"

Lucy smiled deeply. "I love it. I'm extremely nervous, but I love it."

Señora pulled Lucy's arm and urged her to sit with her. They sat close, like two young children about to engage in the whispers of the youth.

"Where are you going tonight? Who is coming? That gentleman who pays for your room?"

"Yes, his name is Nicholas. I don't know where he is taking me but we are working together. We are old friends," Lucy added.

Señora smiled. "You like him? *Sí?*"

Lucy started to laugh. "*Sí*, Señora. It's complicated," Lucy added as she took a deep breath. "I have something to confess, Señora."

Señora leaned in even closer as she watched Lucy struggle with her words.

"I'm married," Lucy stated in a hush.

Señora raised her eyes at Lucy and then suddenly looked toward the doorway, where Nicholas stood quietly, watching the two women interact. Señora stood and pulled Lucy up with her and held her into a strong embrace. She spoke quietly in her ear. "Chapala is a place for romance, where lovers go and passion exceeds. A place so special, it will steal your heart and set you free, all at the same time. Life is complicated, Miss Lucy, but you have a big heart and love has no bounds or limitations. Live and feel often and without guilt."

Lucy tried hard not to cry, but her eyes watered; she loved Señora and would miss her dearly when she left. She was connected to her spirit, she recognized, and they held a quick and special bond.

Her words were wise and gave Lucy the courage to continue. Lucy hugged her fiercely, not wanting to let go. "Thank you. *Te amo.*"

"*Te amo*," Señora replied as she released her and urged her to go on.

Lucy turned around, facing Nicholas as he approached her. She watched his eyes as his expression changed, one from a friendly observer to that of a tortured eyewitness. She could feel his spirit pull on her so deeply, it caught her breath.

She smiled, nervous. She did not want her skin to reveal the heat that she felt between them. She did not want her eyes to reveal the feelings she had for this man she had thought of so many times. But Nicholas was strong and he always protected her, in many more ways than one. He set her at ease with his calm and commanding way.

"Lucy, you look beautiful."

She nodded at him and smiled. Approaching him, she stood by his side, her hand searching for his. She grasped on to it and held it tight.

He squeezed her hand and together they walked out of the hotel lobby, with Señora at their back, blessing them. Quietly she stated, "Take the Lord with you, always."

# CHAPTER 35

*Lucy*

Lucy followed Nicholas past the lobby doors and out onto the street, where he pulled her toward his vehicle. He opened her door and she graciously got in. After he shut it behind her, he walked across the front of his car. She gaged his face as he scanned the surrounding area. He looked serious and distracted, that easygoing attitude that she had just witnessed seemed to be dissipating and Lucy knew that this was all business. She took a deep breath. It was time to work and she needed to feel things; she needed to help him and tonight was the night.

Nicholas sat behind the steering wheel and started the vehicle. He turned toward Lucy with his hand held on the shifter. "Are you ready?" he asked her.

Lucy took a deep breath. "Yes Nicholas, I think so." Lucy crossed her legs toward Nick and lifted her soft fitted dress, confidently revealing the concealed weapon strapped to the inside of her thigh. Nicholas smiled deeply, nodding in agreement. She could feel his pride for her. Nicholas leaned in a little closer and grabbed Lucy's face lightly by her chin. His eyes pierced hers and his energy was powerful, leaving Lucy breathless as she remained still, waiting for his command.

"You realize we aren't going to dinner?" he asked her.

"I do now, yes."

Nicholas smiled. "Whatever happens, Lucy, I want you to stay near me—at all times. Okay? Do not get lost among the natives. Do not think that you will know better than me, what you should do. You need to watch me and look for my directive always. Do you understand?" Nicholas' face was serious and demanding, and Lucy could feel her chest rising and falling as she tried to breathe, his face only inches from hers.

"Nick," she whispered, "I understand." Lucy could feel Nicholas hesitate and she held her breath. She was sure he was going to kiss her, but he pulled away. He was agitated, and she sank back as Nicholas pulled away from the curb and into the street.

"I have this feeling Nick, about Anthony that I just can't shake," Lucy started a few minutes later. Nicholas looked over at her, interested in what she was about to say. "He's regretful. It feels like he's trying to fix his life. I'm pretty sure that he didn't have anything directly to do with the attack on your family home, and if

215

he did indirectly, he's not aware of it." Lucy needed some answers. She wanted to know the history between Anthony and Nicholas; she needed to know what their connection was. "He has strong feelings toward you, regretful feelings. Does any of this make sense?"

Lucy could feel Nick's anxiety. He pressed down on the gas pedal, the car moving faster than before as they made their way onto the freeway.

Nicholas took a deep breath. "To the extent that I don't want to share everything I know about this case with you, for security reasons, I can tell you that Anthony and I were very close growing up together. He was my best friend."

Lucy eyed him. "Okay, so what happened? What changed?"

"You know that Anthony worked for Mr. Garcia. He had once been a respectful businessman; he had everything going for him until he met that murdering son of a bitch." Nicholas paused and glanced over at Lucy. "Anthony immersed himself into Garcia's clique and lived this certain lifestyle. He was sucked into the power of money and influence; it was all I could do to keep him out of it. I tried desperately. We fought, we argued, we even got into physical altercations, but the pull was too powerful for him. He chose a much different direction in life than I did…and then one day, our paths met again and I was forced to investigate him for his illegal activity. Eventually I arrested him and he was charged with

216

drug trafficking and the attempted murder of a police officer." Nicholas exited off the freeway, down a ramp and across a waterway into a more desolate part of town.

Lucy nodded, finally putting all the pieces together. "He's sorry Nick, I truly believe that." Nick continued to drive.

Staying in the town of Chapala, Lucy had the pleasure of experiencing a wonderful, more tourist-driven vacation atmosphere. Everything was lovely, the people were beautiful, the town clean and appealing. Where Nick and she were now was a whole different feel. Just five miles out of town, Lucy could see that not everyone in Mexico experienced the same luxuries she'd seen in Chapala. Garbage littered the sides of the freeway; graffiti was scrolled all over the concrete retaining walls, underpasses, and bridges. She supposed it wasn't much different than visiting some of the inner cities of the United States, but she was surprised at how dissimilar it was on the outskirts of town, and how sheltered she had been in Chapala.

"Where are we going, Nick?" she asked as she watched from her window, observing the buildings they passed and the people on the streets.

"We have surveillance going with an individual called 'Hombre,' who is particularly interested in Anthony—what he does and where he goes. He works with Anthony, but I think that he's been sent in as a spy. I have a feeling that this guy works for Garcia." Nick pulled into a parking lot at the back of a building and parked the car. He turned around and looked from one end of the lot to the other. Lucy glanced behind her at the back of a restaurant where several men were gathered, smoking cigarettes.

"The Hombre frequents this restaurant after work and I have a feeling that Garcia may meet him here today, to gather his information."

Lucy considered the building and the restaurant and the men standing around. She wouldn't fit in, that was clear. She had wished she worn something different.

She looked back at Nick, her face scrunched while she thought aloud. "Could Garcia recognize you?" she asked.

Nick glanced over at her. "Yeah, it's possible. It's been a long time though, I'm sure he has forgotten what I look like." He paused for a moment and stared, puzzled, an expression on him Lucy had never seen before.

"Nick, how could you be so sure? If Anthony is responsible for the break-in at your house, which is what you believe, how would it be that Garcia wouldn't be able to recognize you? The two were in cahoots together for years. I don't think you've thought this through." A smile spread across Lucy's face. She sat back, pleased with her argument and content in the fact that Nicholas was

218

considering what she was saying. "I mean, what *is* your plan?" she went on. "Are you planning on going into that restaurant with me, to watch what you think might be a private meeting between the Hombre and Garcia? If so, is that the best plan you have? Because I'm feeling that Garcia not only knows who you are, but has the image of what you look like etched into his memory."

Nicholas looked into Lucy's face as she spoke, nodding his head.

"You're right—I'm recognizable."

"I will go in," Lucy stated confidently.

Just as the words escaped her mouth, Nick's phone rang.

"Hey Alex," he said as he picked it up.

Lucy sat quietly as Nick spoke on the phone.

"Okay Alex, thanks. I'll handle it." Nick hung up.

"Garcia is here; he just entered the building from the front entrance. He's surrounded by five men," Nick relayed to Lucy. "He is a short man with very dark hair, a very bad comb-over too. He's a little heavyset and dresses like he belongs in a golf tournament."

Lucy nodded. "I know, I remember the photographs." She paused. "So are you going to let me handle this?"

"Yes, but—"

"I'll be fine, Nick. I know what to do."

"I know Lucy, it's just that…before you go inside, I wanted to thank you. For being here. I wanted to tell you this morning, how grateful I am to you, but—"

"Nick, honestly, I'm so relieved that I am able to repay you for all you have done for me and my family. This job has been good for me, personally. Jack's having a real hard time with Pop gone and financially, we need the money. You're helping me just the same and…I needed this time. To sort through some things."

Lucy raised her eyes to Nick's. They both waited as seconds passed. Lucy could feel his energy pull on her, as it always did.

"How is it with Jack? Are you two okay?"

Lucy's heart dropped at the mention of her husband's name. She didn't know how she felt about him anymore. He was always so angry with her.

"We'll figure it out, Nick. It's hard…I'm sure you understand. You have a wife and a family. It's…challenging at times."

Nick nodded and looked down at his watch. "We don't have much time here, but I wanted to tell you that I've never been able to forget about you. You've always been in my thoughts. I've always worried for you. It never stopped for me."

Lucy shook her head, her eyes soft. She was soundly aware that her dreams and the onset of her unfaithful private thoughts had for months been preparing her for this moment. She felt tortured over her feelings for Nick. She hesitated, considered maybe ignoring her instincts, but she couldn't. He was important to her; he was a part of her.

"Nick, I haven't forgotten either. Our time together was special to me and I know this seems crazy, but…I need you. I've always needed you in my life, even if it's just a little piece of you."

Placing his hand along the back of her hair, Nick moved her close to him, and gently he kissed her lips.

Lucy was shocked at the sudden onset of affection from him, but she did not stop him or complain; instead, she placed her hands on his chest and brushed her face along his neck, breathing the smell of his manly aftershave. She could feel his body tense from her touch, smiling at the effect she had on him. She whispered to him, "I think I should go now."

"Lucy, I don't—"

Placing her lips one last time on his mouth, she silenced him briefly, then exited the vehicle before he could object further.

221

She looked across the street at the other unmarked vehicle, grateful that Alex and Carlos was also with them. She felt an additional boost of courage and security as she made her way up the sidewalk to open the front door.

The hallway entrance was dark and narrow. She walked the six-foot lobby toward another doorway opening and stood in front of the reception area. Patrons were scattered about as her eyes scanned the large and dark room. Low chandeliers hung from the tiled ceiling, offering an orange glow over the décor of the restaurant, which was outdated and in need of a makeover. Tattered black booths lined the far wall and an old jukebox sat in the corner. A few men were playing cards at one table and it looked like some questionable women were soliciting near the bar. Garcia and his men convened at the other end of the bar and were quietly speaking to one another. No one seemed to notice Lucy as she slipped into a side booth and opened her phone to call Nick.

She hit redial and waited until he answered. A waitress appeared with her pen and pad and looked Lucy over as she rolled her eyes. It was apparent that waitressing wasn't quite her thing.

"*¿Qué quieres beber?*" she asked.

"English?" Lucy inquired. The waitress rolled her eyes again.

"Can I get you anything to drink?"

"Yes, actually, I'll have a glass of Coke please. I am meeting a friend for dinner, so I'll wait to order until he gets here."

The waitress shrugged and walked away, not appearing to care about the details of Lucy's evening plans.

Nicholas answered the phone. "You drive me crazy! I thought that we agreed, you would listen to me. Didn't we talk about this earlier? I thought you understood."

"We were wasting time, Nick. Although I enjoyed very much our conversation, it was time for me to leave. I'm sitting in a booth anyway, and I can see the men clearly. They have their backs toward me, enjoying drinks. Garcia is here, in the far corner. His phone constantly rings. He seems annoyed by this."

"I want you to get up now and walk out of the building."

"Don't be ridiculous. I'm fine. So what do you want me to do now? What is it that you need to know?"

Nicholas groaned with frustration. Lucy could hear him suffering, but she knew he could do nothing about it.

"Please Nick, I'm fine. I'm not here to hurt you, I'm only here to help you."

"We are waiting for the Hombre. When he gets here, I will let you know."

"Okay, Nick," Lucy said as she continued to stare toward the bar. She noticed she had eyes on her, that she was no longer being ignored. Someone was watching her, not because she was suspicious, but because he liked what he saw. It was an awkward and uncomfortable stare, the way the man was glaring; his face was serious and dangerous looking. She shifted in her seat and moved into the booth a little bit farther to hide herself from her admirer.

"Lucy? Are you still there?" Nick asked.

Lucy cleared her throat. "Yes Nick. I'm here." She tried to restrain from sounding concerned but was uncertain if she came across that way.

"Lucy, the Hombre is here. He's just pulled in. I think he will enter the building shortly. He's a young, strong kid. He's wearing a baseball cap and running shorts."

"Okay, Nick."

"Once he enters, I want you to watch him and tell me if he approaches Garcia. I want to know how long they speak and if they exchange anything physical. Just tell me everything you observe."

"Okay Nick, he's here now. He's just entered." Lucy reached for the dinner menu and pretended to be reading it while she raised her eyes to view what was happening. The young Hombre had approached the bar but sat by himself in the middle. The man who was eyeing her suddenly turned his attention toward the young man and nodded to acknowledge him. The silky ladies at the other end of the bar also took note of the young man and one of them made her way toward him. The woman brushed her body against his back.

The young man recoiled from her as the scary man with the serious eyes and dangerous face shuffled her away.

"*Vamanos*!" he stated gruffly as he rudely waved her off. He then proceeded to sit down next to the young Hombre, and without affection, he shook his hand and pulled him close so that he could whisper something to him. The young man did not look pleased. Few words were spoken and then the young man turned and walked out of the building.

"He's leaving, Nick," Lucy reported into the phone. "He literally sat for one minute, spoke to a big burly man and then got up and walked out. I don't know what else to tell you. Nothing seemed to happen."

Lucy was about to get up and walk out herself when she noticed that the other gentleman—the one who had been staring at her—was approaching her. Lucy put on an unfriendly smile in an attempt to make it clear to him that she was uninterested. He sat down anyway, across from her at the table. Lucy could feel the palms of her hands begin to sweat. She rubbed her thighs together so she could feel her weapon, sure that she would never be brave enough to use it. She cleared her throat. "Is there something I can do for you?" she asked.

The man stared at her languidly. He grabbed Lucy's cell phone and turned it off, placing it in his pocket.

"Excuse me!" she huffed. She tried to grab it back but he took hold of her wrist, squeezing it tight. His skin had been darkened from years of working in the sun, the wrinkles around his eyes were deep, and his crooked smile revealed that he had a tooth or two missing. A pack of cigarettes was tucked deeply into his shirt pocket and he smelled like earth. The tattoos that were etched on both sides of his arms were faded and ancient. *What kind of life did this man lead that brought him here, in this moment, to sit across from me at a table?*

The waitress placed Lucy's glass of Coke in front of her. Lucy wanted to scream to the unfriendly waitress for help, but it didn't seem likely that she would help her. The man's creepy smile turned Lucy's stomach as he crassly ordered the barmaid to bring him another beer.

"If you don't excuse me, I think I'll be leaving now." Lucy attempted to stand up. The man reached across the table, grabbed her arm, and pulled her down into her seat.

"Why don't you just stay right where you are."

"I'm sorry," Lucy started with anger, "have we met?" Lucy's face was flush with warmth as she tried to think about how she was going to dodge this guy. "Are you under some type of impression that I need to listen to you? Because if you are, I'm sorry, you're going to be rightly disappointed. Now, if you don't mind, I'll be going now."

The gruff man reached for her and dragged her into the booth with him. He wrapped his arm around her waist and spoke forcibly into her ear. "You're not going anywhere."

Lucy closed her eyes and prayed. She wasn't sure what to do. If she reached for her gun and threatened this guy, Garcia and his men were certainly going to intervene. She didn't have her phone for Nicholas' help, and besides, she didn't want to prove him right.

"Listen, I'm sorry if I gave you the wrong impression," she said, taking a new approach. "I'm here to meet a friend of mine. He should be here any minute. If he sees me with another man, he may lose his mind and I have no idea what he's capable of." Lucy pushed herself away as far as she could and tried to untangle herself from his arms.

She glanced up toward the doorway, her escape. It was only across the room, fifteen feet. She could make it if she ran, but then what? It was going to cause a scene, and now Alex was probably already following the Hombre who had left.

Lucy took a deep breath. Once more she glanced up—and this time she saw Carlos walk through the entranceway. She felt relieved and looked at him. His concern for her was evident and in the short amount of time they had spent together, Lucy knew that he wasn't going to disappoint her. Carlos walked past the booth and then paused and looked back at the man with the broken teeth.

"*¿Que pasa?*" he asked as he reached across the table to grab the man's hand. In doing so, Carlos intentionally knocked over Lucy's glass of Coke, spilling the dark beverage across the table and onto the floor. Lucy jumped to avoid the sudden onset of fluid, leaving her captor to bear the brunt of the mess.

Carlos continued to be obnoxious in his enthusiasm to reintroduce himself to his alleged old friend. "*¿Qué onda güey? Hace mucho tiempo.*" he asked. The burly man busied himself with a pile of napkins and dabbed angrily at his wet pants.

"*Hola chica!*" Carlos stated as he reached out to Lucy with his hand, embracing her into a fierce hug. "Miss Lucy," Carlos whispered, "it's time for you to go."

Lucy held on to Carlos and then pushed him away from her, giving him and the man an awfully disgusted look. She then turned and walked toward the door as classy as she could. She could hear the men behind start to argue but their voices faded as she reached the front entrance and stepped outside.

Nicholas' car pulled up alongside her. Breathing a sigh of relief, she jumped into the vehicle and they sped down the street. She took a deep breath and turned her attention to Nicholas.

He looked at her sideways. Her stomach turned.

"You're going back to the hotel," he stated.

Lucy sighed.

"I'm sorry," she whispered. She closed her eyes and she prayed for the safety of her friend Carlos. She glanced up at Nicholas again and his face remained unchanged. He was angry. He was hard on her, always. He was just starting to be vulnerable, but now he'd changed, serious again. He affected her deeply and she wanted to make it right.

"Please Nick, I'm sorry."

He ignored her.

# CHAPTER 36

## *Anthony*

Anthony marched into his house, his son Jase a quick step behind him complaining, "Why are you walking so fast, Dad?"

Anthony turned on the young boy, taking in a sharp breath of air to stifle the panic that he felt. "Listen buddy," he started calmly, "I need you to pack a few things in a little bag. Pack a change of clothes, a toothbrush, and pajamas. You're going to stay at Grandma's house tonight, okay? Daddy needs to talk to Mommy for a little bit, so why don't you run into your room now and do as I ask."

Jase walked toward his bedroom and paused in the hallway, looking back at his father like he wanted to argue but deciding he'd better listen. Anthony gave him one last look of encouragement, a half weak smile and then continued to walk through the house, looking for Rose.

Anthony entered his bedroom and found Rose folding laundry on the bed. He thought about his words, fearing her reaction. He hesitated. She looked at him and smiled.

"How'd it go?" she asked. "Did my handsome boy score any goals?" Rose moved around the room, passing Anthony playfully. She kissed him.

Anthony walked over to the bed and sat down. He was delaying, knowing that she wasn't going to enjoy this conversation, but he felt urgency and he didn't want to waste any of their time trying to sugarcoat anything.

"Rose, we need to talk," he started, his tone serious.

Rose had her back toward him but she turned slowly. Nervously, she smiled, as though she thought perhaps he had just made a funny joke or that he was getting ready to tease her, like he always did. Anthony could feel the anxiety in the room as she moved toward the bed to sit down beside him. She reached for his hand.

"I was down at the field when I received the phone call," he said. "It was Garcia. He wants to meet with me tomorrow. When I left the house today, a car was parked across the street. I believe that they followed me."

Rose stood from the bed and went to the window, looking outside toward the street. She reached for the blinds and pulled them down over the glass, darkening the room. She turned and went to the other window, repeating her action. She then went to her dresser and pulled open the bottom drawer. She emptied the clothing onto the floor and reached inside to open another hidden compartment. She pulled out a small handgun, then placed it on the tabletop. She turned and looked at her husband. "Now what?"

"Jase is packing. I want him somewhere safe. I want you to bring him to your parents."

"Yes, okay, but then what?"

"We need to leave town, Rose. We can't stay here."

Rose shook her head adamantly.

"Garcia will never be satisfied until I am either dead or working for him again," Anthony pressed. "I can't do either one, Rose. We have no choice."

"We can stay and fight. It's not reasonable that we be forced to leave the town that we love so much, to move our family around, hiding. They will always find us, Anthony. We can't keep running."

"It's too risky. What if something happens to us, what about Jase?"

Anthony moved off the bed, went to his wife, and held her by the shoulders.

"You need to be here for him. You are his life, you are his mother. I can't let you be a part of this, Rose. You take him to your parents. You stay there until you hear from me. I will face Garcia and I will defend myself. This is my fight, not yours."

Rose grabbed hold of her husband and held him tight. "I'm nothing without you Anthony, please, I want to help you."

Anthony continued to shake his head no, aware that Rose was stubborn. He needed to convince her that she needed to stay with her son.

"Please Rose, you need to trust me. If I'm worrying about you, then there will be mistakes made. I need to focus and be alert; it's better this way. You need to understand."

Rose lowered her eyes to the floor as the magnitude of what was happening settled in. She began to cry.

Anthony squeezed his wife's body, afraid to let her go as if he may never see her again. He stopped and looked down into her face; he kissed her mouth. "I love you, Rose. I will come home to you, I promise. We will be a family and we will be free."

Rose nodded and wiped at her tears with the back of her hand. She walked over to the dresser and placed the small handgun in her bag. Approaching the doorway she paused, looking back at Anthony, one last time.

"*Te amo mucho*, my sweet boy."

Anthony closed his eyes, took a deep breath and when he opened them again, she was gone.

# CHAPTER 37

## *Anthony*

Anthony unlocked the back door of his home and walked outside. He could feel the stress lines etched across his forehead as he thought about the phone call he received from Mr. Garcia. The fact that his former "employer" was eager to meet with him the following day only meant one thing: that they were coming for him tonight. Anthony knew that he would never survive such a meeting and was beginning to have regrets about the choices he made. He shouldn't have come back to Mexico; he should have moved his family to the United States where they would be safe, but the immigration process was difficult and time consuming.

Anthony's hands shook. His instincts were on high alert as he scanned the yard for any unusual activity. His movements were sharp and purposeful as he entered the small shed in the corner lot of his property. Moving to the back of the tiny building, he took out a small set of keys. He unlocked the oversized metal containers intended for yard equipment and children's toys. Inside was a variety

235

of handguns, a collection Anthony had made during the course of his career. He grabbed three that he felt would suit him well and placed them on his body—one along his leg, one on the inside of his vest, and one near his hip. He also had a bulletproof vest. He put his arms inside the heavy piece of equipment and strapped it to his chest.

He would go to the festival. He knew that he would be followed. He suspected that he was being watched and hoped to lead the men into a situation where the opportunity to defend himself would best benefit him. That was his plan.

After he was armed adequately, he returned to his vehicle and started to make his way downtown, toward the city celebration. The area was crowded, parking difficult but he found a secured lot one mile from the fairgrounds. The festival was a joyous occasion; children laughed and squealed, running around from one parent to the other. The alleyways were packed with patrons and vendors, which made walking through the crowd difficult and claustrophobic. Anthony managed to make his way, suspicious of every passerby, keenly eyeing the crowd as he looked around the festival.

He walked toward the food concession. The smells of the Mexican cuisine reminded him that he hadn't eaten anything today. His stomach soured at the idea, his nerves sharp like small stab wounds all along his body. He walked past the mariachi singers playing festival music in the aisles. He inspected the vendors as they displayed their breads and spices, articles of clothing, and crafts, hoping to recognize the men that he feared were searching for him. Turning around often, he felt a gentle breeze blow against the back of his neck; an eerie feeling seemed to fill the air as the voices around him became silent.

He continued outside of the festival to the cobblestone streets of Chapala. The sounds of festival music faded behind him; the night sky was dark and lit with stars and ancient clouds.

Instinctively he understood that it was time. His hands were sweaty with perspiration; the adrenaline that pumped through his veins was a feeling that he recognized and felt comfortable with. This was not his first gun battle, and hopefully it wouldn't be his last.

Anthony turned the corner and headed for the marina. He looked behind him—no one. He reached into his inside belt pocket and removed a small firearm and carried it at the side of his hip.

The alleyway was dark when two men appeared, each silhouette shadowed by the small lampposts that sporadically lined the blackened passage. The men's stature revealed menacing behavior, their strength and authority concerning, but Anthony was relieved to recognize that there were only two men.

The two figures continued up the cobbled street toward him; he knew they were possibly armed. He grabbed his gun and

237

began shooting. The deafening noise of the gunfire echoed down the narrow alley, fading up along the sides of the tall buildings and out into the dark sky.

Anthony's hunch was right: The men returned fire, forcing Anthony to dodge the assault by jumping behind a dumpster.

"¡No mames!" they yelled, his quick strike on them somewhat a surprise as they scrambled to take cover. He waited, crouching down into an awkward position, his legs burning as he peeked beyond the metal container. He held his gun and reloaded, ammunition dropping to the ground as he hurried. Aggressively he fired off another round, a rain of sparks flying over head as shots ricocheted off the dumpster.

One man screamed, "¡Alanzo! ¡Me han disparado!" The man held his chest, fell to the ground and landed in a muddied puddle of water. Behind the men, another round of shots fired off, catching the last of the assailants off guard. He was shot in the back and dropped to his knees next to his partner.

Anthony couldn't see the shooter, but was thankful for the assistance. He waited with his gun drawn until he could see the figure more clearly. The assailant's shoes echoed throughout the alleyway as Anthony's rescuer sauntered up the cobbled drive. As the figure approached, Anthony saw it was a woman. Her walk was deliberate, recognizable, her confidence admirable. Anthony lowered his weapon and watched as the beauty made her way toward him. As she approached, Anthony couldn't help but feel pride for her. She was the most incredible woman he had ever known.

"Rose, how did you find me?" He grabbed her by the waist and pulled her close.

"I never left you," she replied confidently. Anthony hesitated then kissed Rose forcibly on the lips. Rose tilted her head back and looked up at her husband. "I couldn't bear it if something happened to you."

Anthony paused, lingering. He stared into her eyes and felt his breath catch as he considered what his wife had done for him. They were a team, and she had his back. It was still hard for him to believe, but she always did. She always had his back.

"Rose. We need to go now," Anthony murmured. She nodded and waited for her husband to make his move. He grabbed her hand and together, they ran through the alley toward the marina. Although he was unsure of what was around the next corner, Anthony was confident that this wasn't over.

It was just the beginning.

# CHAPTER 38

*Lucy*

Nicholas was driving Lucy toward the hotel when the call came in. There was a shooting downtown; two men were dead. Lucy closed her eyes and meditated while Nicholas sped down the highway toward Chapala.

Lucy could see the souls of the two men, dark and shadowed. Shivers went down her arms and a rotten taste filled her mouth. The two men were evil; their lives were not worth crying over. She could feel Anthony and Rose's spirit—they were on the run. Their connection to one another was strong and Lucy marveled at the level of affection that they had for one another. Rose was a proud woman; she loved Anthony.

Lucy tried to see where they were going, but Nick was on the phone, yelling into the receiver and giving direction to his men. His voice was distracting and he was still angry with her, which diverted her thoughts. She placed her hand on his arm while he drove, trying to get his attention with her eyes. He inhaled deeply.

"It's going to be okay, Nick. The two men shot were Garcia's men. Anthony and Rose are on the run. I can still feel them."

"Where are they?" he asked. His voice was rough.

"I don't know, I can't see where they are heading but they are in town. Maybe hiding."

Lucy dropped her eyes to the floor.

"I need to say this, and I want you to listen to me. I like them. I like who they are, Anthony and Rose. They are good people. I don't think that he's involved with you. Not knowingly and not directly, anyway. I think you should try to help them." Lucy could feel her words having a small affect on him; she knew that Nick was fond of Anthony. They were best friends once, when they were young, after all. She knew that he still cared for him.

Nick's stare rattled her, but she met his glare, not wanting to back down to him, feeling strength in her vision and purpose in her message. He broke first, breathing deeply, the muscles in his neck and the veins in his forehead stressed. Lucy prayed for him; she understood that this was difficult for him and that he was thinking about his family.

"I'm going to drop you off," he said.

"*No*, Nick! I'm staying with you. Please! You need me, I can help you."

Nicholas shook his head. He wasn't usually flexible, Lucy knew, but this was very important. She wanted to be there for him; she wanted him to need her.

"Please Nick," she implored. She could see Nicholas was about to argue with her, but abruptly, he relented. Perhaps he felt that she would be safer with him than away from him.

They approached the carnival, where Lucy could see the massive crowds of people. Nick drove around the blocked-off streets, down the small alleyways, away from the crowds. She could see some of Nick's men standing guard at various corners of the roads, hidden in the shadows.

Lucy looked out of the back window. The oversized SUVs that carried Garcia and his men were behind them, riding up on their vehicle and pressuring them to move over. They overcame the car, the two trucks surrounded them on all sides, one taking the lead, speeding recklessly in front of them. Nick started to slow his vehicle and one by one, they drove around him and continued down the road.

"They're not looking for us," Nick muttered.

"Follow them," Lucy instructed. She removed her gun from its hidden holster and loaded it.

"This isn't a good idea, Lucy." Nick pulled over. "I want you to get out here. You can walk to the festival and then take a cab over to the hotel. This will be far too dangerous for you."

She sighed, angry at the time that was ticking away. "Nick, I'm not leaving. Pick up the phone and call Alex."

Nick sighed and then reached for his phone. "Alex, Garcia's men just passed us. They're riding in the same two large black SUVs as they were earlier. They are heading toward the marina. I'm going to follow them and hand Lucy the phone. She can update you as we make our way down."

Nicholas handed the phone to Lucy and then placed his palm on the side of her face. He reached in and kissed her delicately. "Please, be careful," he said. Lucy closed her eyes and absorbed his energy. The intensity of the situation along with Nick's attention was going to drive her insane. Never, ever would she experience anything like this again.

He turned his attention back to driving the vehicle. She spoke into the phone, "Hey Alex, is Carlos okay? I just wanted to thank him for his help at the restaurant."

"He's okay, Lucy. I just spoke with him; he's with the others now. Waiting."

Nick pulled his vehicle alongside the road behind the hotel where he stayed. He grabbed the phone from Lucy.

"Alex, we're going to move by foot now. I'm going to head south on Route One and then search the side streets. Why don't you do the same coming toward me and then we'll meet in the middle?"

Alex agreed. Lucy opened her door and stepped out into the street. Nick stopped her one last time to give her direction. "I don't care what is happening—if you hear gunshots, I want you to hide. Do you understand? You take cover, Lucy, and don't come out until I find you."

"Yes, Nicholas. I understand."

"Okay, let's go." He grasped her hand in his and they moved down the street. Nicholas wrapped his arm around her and pulled her in close as he scanned the vicinity and the alleyways. Lucy understood that Nick was trying to look natural, as if they were a couple out for a romantic stroll. She loved the feel of his arm around her.

The phone rang. After a few moments of hushed conversation, Nick hung up.

"That was Alex," he said to Lucy. "He found Garcia. They're parked over at the corner of Route One and Beach Avenue. He has Carlos and Miguel stationed over there now, pretending to be fisherman. They're looking for Anthony. He's got to be around here, somewhere. If they find him first, we'll never get the answers we need." His mouth formed a hard line. "We have to find Anthony."

The long, narrow road ran along Chapala Lake. Lucy could see the boats moving with the currents and could hear the waves slapping against the docks, but it was dark and difficult to see the water. Small boutiques and little coffee shops lined the walkway. She wished she had visited the area in the daylight, romantic and beautiful as it seemed.

Up ahead, Lucy noticed lights and a patron leaving a pastry shop. The patron passed them, nodding hello. Nick and Lucy walked toward the lighted store and glanced into the window. Anthony and Rose were there, sitting quietly at a table for two, enjoying a cup of coffee and pastry. They sat and they smiled at each other, as if there were no danger, nothing to worry about. Lucy wanted to run inside and warn them, to tell them to get going, to ask them why were they just sitting there?

Nicholas took a deep breath. "He never understood. He was always so careless. He has no idea now."

"What are you going to do, Nick?" Lucy asked. "I think we should go in there and talk with them."

He scoffed. "He can't be reasoned with, Lucy. Don't think for one second that he won't try to kill me, because he will."

The thought that Nick could die turned Lucy's stomach. Distracted at his words, she thought about her family and Jack and the dangerous situation she had put herself in. Maybe she should have gone back to the hotel and waited, but she was scared for Nicholas. She didn't want to lose him.

"So what should we do?" she asked.

"We'll wait and follow them. Eventually, we'll all come together."

Nick pulled Lucy into the dark alleyway. Minutes later, Rose and Anthony were on the move again; this time, they were in a much bigger hurry.

Nick was armed and ready. He waited until Anthony and Rose were at least one block ahead of them, and then they followed the couple. Anthony kept pivoting his head, obviously alert, watching his surroundings. Several times Anthony had looked straight at Nick and Lucy, but did not appear to recognize them.

Nick's phone rang. Lucy could see him nodding. Alex was undoubtedly on the other line, informing him. She waited until the call ended and looked at Nick questioningly.

"There are ten men in total," Nick informed her. "They are dispersing in two groups, five men in each. They are heading north toward us, one group on Route One, the other parallel on Chapala Avenue. They are armed. Our men are coming in behind us. They'll be in pairs. Garcia's men are dressed in black, and our country boys have their cowboy hats on. There are a lot of players here, and I don't want to mistake any of our men for theirs."

As they rounded the next block, Lucy could see Anthony up ahead, speaking to Rose, his arm wrapped around her waist as they walked.

Sudden gunfire echoed off the tall buildings.

Sparks and flames rained overhead as Anthony and Rose ducked out of the way, the gunfire just missing them and hitting the metal sign above them. The two started to run.

Nicholas drew his gun, running after Anthony and Rose and down the street. Lucy followed cautiously.

Anthony and Rose disappeared up a side alley. Nick slowed, his gun drawn, Lucy following behind him. They walked gingerly, ducking behind vehicles and doorways, walking with quick paces through emptiness.

More gunfire echoed up ahead. Nick and Lucy ran toward the sound, which rang again to the right of them, and found the alleyway suddenly congested with men at either side. Nick stopped and turned to Lucy.

"Listen to me, I want you to run!" He spun her around and pointed toward a small opening between the walls of an adjacent building. Lucy looked through space. She could make it through with ease, but Nicholas was much bigger than she was. He would have a hard time, and she didn't want to go alone. She looked back at him, her eyes big with fear, her heart racing as more gunfire erupted around them. "Go Lucy, go!" Nicholas yelled.

She ran, wedging herself through the narrow passageway, praying the entire time she moved. She looked back once or twice for Nick, but he was gone.

She removed her firearm and held it in her shaking hands. Feeling desperate, the dark shadows chasing her, she passed through the alley, a forceful breeze breathing down her neck, hurrying her along to get to the other side. She jumped over garbage cans, skated past fire escape ladders, and clambered through debris until she reached the end.

Pausing, she panted, looking both ways before stepping out onto the abandoned street. She wasn't sure where she was supposed to run toward, but she figured away from the gunfire was a good start. She removed her heels and tossed them aside, cursing at herself once again for wearing such a ridiculous outfit to her alleged dinner with Nicholas. She could hear the men shouting and yelling, police sirens were approaching as she moved along the street.

Her heart was exploding out of her chest. She prayed. She thought about her children, feeling the devastation rip through her heart at the thought of never seeing them again. Overcome with emotions, she paused to catch her breath and to get her bearings.

It was in that one moment she saw her—Rose—coming out from the shadows of the streets, standing still in silence, looking at Lucy as if she had seen a ghost or perhaps just someone she knew, a spirit of her heart. Lucy stared back, once again in awe at Rose's stunning beauty. She longed to run to her, to run with her, to help the men they loved and to return them all home to their families. She waited, holding to her firearm.

Anxiety rang throughout her body like a fire alarm. It was hard to manage what she was feeling; her intuitive spirit was overcome physically. Lucy's legs gave out under her and her knees buckled. Rose rushed forward, catching her before she hit the stone street.

"Oh, the woman with the dress." Rose looked surprised.

"I'm sorry, Rose," Lucy gasped. "But it's Anthony; he's in very bad danger. I wanted to help him."

"*Si*, I know," Rose stated. She lifted Lucy to her feet. "Are you okay?"

"Yes, I think so." Lucy could hear the chaos still erupting on the next street when she noticed that Rose was bleeding on her left arm. "Your arm?" Lucy asked.

"I was shot earlier, trying to help my husband. The bullet just grazed me...I'm fine, it's just a little blood. Are you ready, can you move now? We need to find him. I can't leave here without him," Rose said, panic etched on her face.

Lucy focused on the problem. She didn't want to return back to the other street, but Rose needed her help and Lucy needed to help her.

She pulled Rose back through the narrow passageway, back toward the fighting and the chaos. They ran together, hand in hand, each of them sharing the same look of concern. They stood at the entrance to the other side and looked out onto the alleyway. Several bodies lay lifeless along the road. Lucy looked for Nick, hoping he was not among them.

Two black SUVs pulled up at the opposite end of the alleyway as three men jumped inside. "*Vamanos! Vamanos!*"

The police were coming, the sirens were getting louder, and Lucy could see that most of the men who remained unharmed were dispersing into the shadows again, not wanting to be seen or identified.

Rose stepped out into the street, her stride purposeful and elegant. She moved through the bodies. Lucy followed her, looking upon the many empty faces. The spirits of their souls surrounded her energy like bees around honey. She could barely breathe.

Rose spoke, "No...no, no!" she cried, running toward Anthony, his body lying near an abandoned shopping cart. She fell on him. Screaming, she moved his head into her lap. She rubbed his face and kissed him, speaking in Spanish. Lucy was incapable of interpreting her words but could feel her sorrow and passion as she cried.

Lucy ran to Rose and knelt beside her as Rose buried her face in her husband's neck. Lucy sobbed, saying prayers of healing and praying for his soul. There was nothing she could do for her; she felt helpless.

"I'm sorry Rose, I'm so sorry," Lucy whispered. Rose was inconsolable, her devastation shattering Lucy's spirit.

Lucy held to Rose for a moment then stood from the street. Her heart was broken; she didn't know what to do but walk and maybe try for help. She started to run again; through the alleyway she went, back to the other side where maybe she could find someone to assist them. That's when she saw them—Nick and Carlos, they were looking for her. She ran to Nick and jumped into his arms.

"You're okay! You're okay!" She stopped again and looked at him closer. "Are you okay?" she asked with tears in her eyes.

"I'm okay, come on, let's go."

"Wait, Nick…Anthony…he needs help."

"It's too late for Anthony. He's gone. Come on, we need to go!"

Lucy heard his words but she didn't want to believe them. Nicholas pulled her along the road, forcing her to move with him, holding her by her arm and dragging her away from the alleyway and back to the vehicle that was waiting for them. Lucy was too stunned to argue. She wanted things to end differently. She would never forgive herself for leaving Rose alone to cry over Anthony and speak her words of love and despair.

She would never forget her.

She cried for Rose.

# CHAPTER 39

## *Jack*

Jack sat on his couch, watching his brother Charles gather his things as he prepared to leave the house. The relationship between the two of them had been strained and Jack wanted to make things right again.

"Charles, do you have a sec?"

"I'm in a big hurry, Jack. What's up?" Charles stood at the front door, his hand on the doorknob.

"I wanted to apologize. I know the men were a little intense at the meeting the other night, and I know that my change in attitude probably came as a bit of a surprise to you."

Charles took a step forward, no longer in a big hurry; he stood facing Jack and listened to his words.

"I hope you understand where I'm coming from."

"Jack, I don't. I don't understand a lot of the things that you do, but if you don't want to search for Pop's killer anymore, that's your business. What I decide to do with my time is my business. We don't have to work together on this one. We'll just work our farm and see what happens."

Jack was quick to his feet, facing his older brother. He had a hard time accepting the fact that Charles considered the farm "his farm" and the use of "us" and "ours" irritated Jack. He needed to be clear to him—crystal clear.

"Charles…where do you see yourself in a couple of years? Do you plan to go back east, back to commercial fishing? I mean, I do appreciate all that you've done here, but I hate to keep you from your life. I know how much you love fishing." Jack stared at his brother, his face stern and his eyes unwavering.

Charles met his stare with unrested eyes, his face drawn as if sleep had evaded him for months, his posture combative. "I don't plan to return back east. Not until I feel that you have things under control here, Jack. I want to stay and help. This is *our* family's legacy; this was where *my* mother grew up and where *my* grandfather made his living. I don't want to see *you* screw this up." Charles glared at Jack as he made his way around him.

Jack could feel his temper begin to rise at his brother's arrogance and assumed self-entitlement. He bit back the words *Go to hell* from his lips. Then he saw it. Something wasn't right here, and Jack was going to find out what that was.

Charles opened the front door. "I have to go now," he stated, pausing for a second. He walked out.

Jack jumped in his car, following in the same direction as his brother, just a few miles down the road behind him. He could see the gray Chevy pickup ahead as Charles pulled into the town garage parking lot. Jack pulled over his vehicle, hung back alongside the road and watched through binoculars as Charles exited his car. Walking over to the town's only payphone, Charles picked up the receiver, emptied quarters onto the small shelf, and placed his phone call.

The first call was quick. A few minutes and the phone call had ended.

The second call was far more energetic. Jack could see Charles was angry as he slammed the phone receiver against the glass door. He argued into the phone and made erratic hand gestures with his fists. Jack thought perhaps Charles had made an enemy or two among the new friends he had met during the meetings. He thought that maybe he was still trying to convince people to continue on with the search for Pop's killer. Either way, his behavior seemed bizarre.

256

Charles walked back to his truck, paused and lit up a cigarette. He looked around suspiciously, then walked toward the town garage side door. He checked first to see if the door was unlocked, which it wasn't. It was a Sunday morning and the streets and garage were empty. There were no other vehicles other than Jack's, and he was parked too far back for Charles to see him.

At first Charles put his weight up against the door to see if it would budge. When it didn't, Charles stood back and kicked the door. After two tries, the door flung open and Charles disappeared behind it. Jack waited for a second and was beginning to think that his brother had lost his mind. He couldn't understand why Charles would break into the garage.

When Charles reappeared again two minutes later, he held a brown paper bag in his hand. He jumped back into his vehicle and sped out of the parking lot.

Jack started his truck and continued to follow him, unsure where he was going next, but definitely not leaving without finding out what his brother was up to.

Charles stopped at the small country store along Route 177. He walked in, grabbed a few groceries then turned around and headed back toward the farm. Jack drove quietly in his truck, trying to remember his brother as a good person, someone that he used to look up to and who he trusted. It had been a long time since he felt that way about Charles. The trust they had when they were young had been shattered when Charles had abandoned Jack after their mother died. Their relationship never had a chance to heal after that; the time they spent together was short and Jack was beginning to question who Charles was as a person.

Charles drove straight for Pop's farm. Jack stopped his vehicle and waited to see what was happening. He watched Charles park his truck. Susie Mae was still at church and Jack knew that she'd be gone all day.

Charles parked his car and made a straight line for the barn, opened the door, and disappeared inside it.

After a few minutes Jack followed to see what the hell he was doing. Making his way along the fence, he hid behind the tree line and waited. His senses urgent, Jack trotted down the stone driveway and entered the barn through a single side door. Passing the empty stalls where the horses used to be, he turned the corner where they had once found pop's lifeless body.

Jack's heart was still heavy with pain every time he entered that barn. The memories were difficult and he hated the feeling of lifelessness now. He thought that someday, when Susie Mae had passed on, maybe he and Lucy would move into the big farmhouse and that they would bring life back into the old barn—a decision that would make Pop happy and proud.

Jack turned the corner to see his brother pulling up a floorboard with a crowbar, the bag to his side. Charles glanced up at Jack, his face bright red with strain, veins bulging in his forehead. Jack eyed the bag as Charles straightened himself, crowbar in hand. He grabbed the bag.

"What's in the bag, Charles?"

"What do you want, Jack?" he spat. "I'm busy here."

Jack walk toward his brother. "What the fuck are you doing, Charles? I just saw you leave the town garage with the bag. What's in the bag?"

Charles rubbed his bearded face defiantly. He managed to never shave. The look was unappealing on him, unkempt and shabby like the way he dressed lately. Charles smiled slightly, menacingly as he casually threw the bag toward his brother, a satisfied look on his face.

Jack caught the bag. He dumped it upside down onto the barn dirt floor, emptying a large, blood-covered mechanical wrench, a tool used for removing large nuts and bolts specific to repairing some of the bigger farming equipment. Jack stared at the heavy device as it landed on the dirt-covered barn floor. A small cloud of dust moved throughout the air, kicked up by the heavy object.

There was a sudden flush of fear as his heart raced. His hands shook, and he was afraid of knowing the truth.

Jack reached down and picked up the tool in his hand, a rush of rage flooding throughout his body. He understood what this meant. Images of his poor grandfather, the trauma to his head entered Jack's mind. He thought of the blood that had pooled around his figure, of picking up his cold body and carrying him to the ambulance. He thought of the helplessness he felt, all these months, how he was unable to save him.

"Surprised, Jack?" Charles asked. "I didn't mean to kill him. He just wouldn't listen and give me what I wanted." Charles paced the floor back and forth, the crowbar still in his hand.

Jack took a few steps forward, his face contorted. He shook his head back and forth. "Charles? What are you saying?"

"It's this farm, Jack," Charles said. "It's evil. This family...I don't belong." Charles paused, straightening his back; he reached for an old bottle of whiskey lying on the floor. He took a deep swig and continued. "The night of the party, I came here. I was drunk...I vaguely remember running into Pop. He threatened me, told me how 'disappointed' he was, blah blah blah." Charles started to laugh. "The old man didn't know what he had coming to him. All I needed was the money; he owed it to me. He just wouldn't listen."

Jack's mouth filled with poison. Months of pain and anger crashed down around him. The lights overhead became blurry. Feeling faint, he took in huge gulps of air to keep from falling to the ground. He held to the wrench, his knuckles bright from exertion. He held strongly to the only weapon he had around him, the same weapon that killed his grandfather.

Charles sneered under his breath. "He was just an old man, Jack. I set you up straight now—the whole farm is fucking yours! Aren't you the lucky one?"

Jack lunged at his brother, tackling him with his full force and slamming him against the tower of hay bales stacked against the wall. Years of working hard on the farm had physically trained Jack and strength was definitely in his favor. Charles was no match. Jack was strong, but emotionally, he was falling apart.

"He was our grandfather, he was our family, you stupid son of a bitch!"

Jack's words were masked in a fury of spittle. He cried through his anger and swung his arms relentlessly.

Charles shoved Jack off of him. He swung his crowbar carelessly in the air, but it was big and clumsy and Jack easily knocked it out of his hand. Jack leaned back off of his brother and punched him hard in the face. Blood splattered everywhere, choking Charles as he tried to gasp for air. He spat.

Jack dragged his brother to his feet and held him by the neck of his shirt with his hand. Cocking his arm back, he punched his brother another time. Blood flowed from Charles' mouth; pieces of teeth flew across the floor. Charles clutched at his mouth and dropped to the ground.

"You're a goddamn pussy," he said, his mouth nothing but blood and loose teeth. "You punch like a girl. Is that all you've got?"

Jack drew himself up, dangerously close to following in his murderous brother's footsteps. "You knew this whole time, you murdering piece of shit." Jack kicked him in the stomach and watched Charles clutch his gut, hunched over like a pile of rubble.

Charles rolled around the barn floor, moaning in pain and helplessly defenseless.

Jack kneeled down next to him, crying. He grabbed a fist full of his hair and twisted Charles' head toward his.

"Tell me why, Charles," he ground out. "Why did you kill him? He was all we had."

Charles showered Jack with a spray of blood as he spoke. "He was all *you* had." Charles hesitated. "I had nobody."

Jack was stunned as he listened to his brother's words. Charles' eyes glazed over, deep-rooted in hate and jealousy. He lay back in silence. Jack dropped to the barn dirt floor, his face wet with tears and dirt, his shirt full of blood and sweat.

He had always thought about killing someone. He had always wanted to kill his mother's murderer, and now Pop's, but he never fathomed that he'd have to kill his own brother. Why was this happening? He couldn't get all evil thoughts out of his mind.

Jack rose to his knees and crawled across the floor to pick up the crowbar. He moved back toward his brother and raised the bar high up over his head. He held it strong, his arms shaking. He looked down at the weak man before him, the drug-addicted, alcohol-crazed, lazy piece of shit brother of his. He thought about how pathetic Charles was to kill an unarmed, elderly man, his grandfather.

"You're a pitiful, useless human being, Charles," he gasped. "I hope you will rot in hell for the pain you caused this family."

Jack wasn't like his brother at all. He lowered his weapon. As much as he hated Charles, he was his brother, flesh and blood.

Jack dropped the bar to the ground and kicked his brother one final time.

"You'll spend a lifetime in jail, Charles. I'll see to it if it kills me."

He turned his back, about to walk away when Charles grabbed hold of his ankle and tripped him to the floor. Charles was up and in one swipe of the crowbar, Jack felt a warm flood of darkness casting shadow over his eyes as his body collapsed with a loud thud.

He was out cold.

# CHAPTER 40

## *Charles*

Charles stood over Jack, wiping away the blood from his mouth. He turned and spit the bright red mucous onto the ground. He gazed over his brother's body, remembering when he was young, having to identify his mother, dead at the morgue. He closed his eyes as the painful reminder of his mother's face flooded his thoughts.

"I'm just like her," he murmured to himself. "The dumb, drug addict slut. I'm just like her."

He pulled out a dirty handkerchief from his back pocket and dabbed gingerly around his nose, trying to stop the bleeding. He glared down at Jack and spoke into the empty air surrounding them.

"You son of a bitch, you had to go and break my nose."

Charles kicked Jack's foot and then walked around and kneeled down beside him to check his pulse. He was still alive.

Charles looked around for the bottle of whiskey. Stumbling, he picked it up off the ground and wiped its mouth clear of dirt and dust. He drank several large gulps until it was gone, welcoming the relief the alcohol offered him. His mind was beginning to cloud with emotion, and he preferred to feel nothing, nothing for his family and for his brother who lay dying at his hands.

He threw the bottle out over the piles of unused milk cartons, then looked around for some rope. He found small pieces of twine used to bundle the hay bales and pulled on them. They were sturdy and unbreakable. He walked over to Jack and turned him on his back, then he took his hands and arms and put them together, then tied the rope into a knot. He repeated the same action with his legs and feet, then dragged Jack through the barn and laid him in one of the empty horse stalls.

He stared at his brother's body.

"I should kill you for being such a spoiled, arrogant asshole."

Charles picked up the crowbar and continued on with the original task of hiding the murder weapon. He pried again at the floorboards, popping the old nails and removing the plank from its space. He looked down into the hole. There was ample room to place the weapon and no one would know any different. He held the large wrench, moving it from one hand to another, side to side he passed. A look of satisfaction made its way across his face.

With Jack out of the picture, Susie Mae didn't have a chance in hell to keep him out of Pop's estate. He was the only one remaining, the last blood relative to Pop—and he deserved it all, everything.

He buried the weapon, stood, and staggered, feeling the full effects of the alcohol coursing through his body. Walking past the stall where Jack lay and toward the front of the barn, he smashed the glass casing of a small gun locker mounted on the wall and lifted the gun out of the holder. His face felt stiff and his jaw rigid. He reached in for a handful of slugs and loaded the gun handily. He felt like his body was no longer his, like his movements were of someone else's, his actions not his own. He placed all the extra ammo in his pocket for safekeeping and then walked back toward Jack. He held the gun by his side, opened the door, and looked in at his brother.

Blood had trickled down the side of Jack's face and made a small puddle by his nose, which lay planted in the dirt. He was still out cold, the wound on his head matting his hair against his skull. Charles leaned down to see if Jack was breathing. He was. He stood and kicked him several times to see if he would move. He didn't.

He lifted his shotgun and took several steps back, then pointed the gun at Jack's head.

"Uncle Charles! Uncle Charles!"

Charles looked up. It was Anna; she was screaming and running straight for the barn, hollering.

"Wait Anna, wait for Aunty. I'm not sure if he's in there," Kat hollered behind her.

Charles lowered the gun by his side and walked out of the horse pen, shutting the stall door behind him. Grabbing his handkerchief, he wiped the blood off his face so Anna wouldn't be too alarmed at the sight of him. He walked toward the door and met Kat and the kids halfway.

Anna took one look at him and yelled, "Oh my gosh, Uncle, what happened to you?"

Charles looked down at his shirt, which was covered in blood, and he could feel that his face was beginning to swell.

Kat stopped short and took Anna by the hand. Sammy was in her arms. "Charles, are you okay?"

"Yeah, yeah, I'm fine. I was pulling on some old milk containers out of the loft and one of them landed on my face. I'm fine though. Come on, let's go to the farmhouse so I can clean up. What are you guys doing down here anyway?"

"Uncle Charles, Uncle Charles, can you come to lunch with us, down at the church?"

"Oh, is that why you're here, Anna?" Charles smiled at little Anna. She had always paid attention to Charles; she was always eager to spend her time with him and showed a genuine concern for his well being. He liked that about her. She was the only one in the family he liked.

"Yes, you have to come! Please! It will be soooo boring if you don't come!"

Charles let out a laugh. "Anna, you always know how to brighten my day. I wish there were more people like you in this world."

"Charles, maybe you should have your nose looked at," Kat said. "It doesn't look very good. You're starting to get black and blue all around your eye."

Charles took the back of his hand and brushed the tip of his nose with it, the throbbing pain jolting his head back.

He took a deep breath and ignored Kat. He continued to walk toward the house, chatting with Anna, when he noticed the bald eagle sitting on the edge of the rooftop, staring down at him, watching them.

"Huh," Charles huffed. He stopped and stared back, then raised his shotgun toward the foul animal.

"Charles!" Kat cried. "What are you doing?"

Charles lowered the shotgun again to his side. "Oh, I'm just kidding, Kat. Right, Anna?"

Anna stared at her uncle, her eyes confused and horrified. She loved animals. She would never hurt an animal and certainly not a bald eagle. She remained silent.

Charles looked at all three of them—Kat, Anna, and Sammy. His mind was racing as to what he should do now.

He continued on toward the house and they all followed him. Walking into the kitchen, he went straight to the refrigerator, grabbed a beer, and opened it. He drank it dry and then grabbed another one. Kat stood in the doorway, Anna at her side.

Charles looked at her, trying to determine if he could muster any feeling for her, any true feeling that would alter his mind and deter him from his task at hand. He couldn't find any.

"Sit down, Kat," he said roughly. Kat stood where she was. Charles raised his weapon again and pointed the gun at her.

"Sit down," he said again, this time with an edge of the anger that he felt deep down inside.

Kat was about to speak. Charles interrupted.

"SHUT IT KAT! Just sit down and shut the fuck up!"

Kat glared at him as she moved across the kitchen and sat at the table with Anna and Sammy at her side. "You're drunk," she spat. "You're always drunk."

He looked up at Kat, who had tears in her eyes, and Anna, whose face had crumpled into terror and confusion. He glared at them all, their judgmental faces looking across the table at him.

"This *is* your fault, Kat. This is all your fault."

# CHAPTER 41

*Lucy*

It was over. Anthony was dead, Garcia was dead, several other men, all dead. She replayed the moment in her mind over and over again. It was like a bad dream, a nightmare that she couldn't wake up from. The bodies lay on the road, lifeless and bloodied. She had expected the violence—she anticipated that the job was not going to be easy—but she never expected to feel so frantic inside. *Rose.* She thought about Rose and she cried; tragic tears burned her eyes. It wasn't fair. She didn't want it to end this way. She wanted Anthony and Rose to live happily ever after.

But this wasn't a fairytale.

She packed her belongings, throwing into the bag her meager clothing, her toiletries, and the gifts for her children. She sat on the edge of the bed and waited for Nick, who had said he would return soon. He didn't want to leave her, she knew, but she didn't think he had a choice.

She had changed back into her old jeans and her comfortable boots, shoving her now-ruined dress back into the bag of her tattered belongings. She wanted to run downstairs into the arms of Señora, and tell her what had happened. She hoped to feel the comfort of the woman she had grown to love so much, but she couldn't. She couldn't move from her bed, so she sat still and waited.

She needed to go home, and she was ready. She prayed she would forget about the trip and settle back into her comfortable life with Jack. She knew she would have some explaining to do, but she hoped that he would forgive her.

Lucy closed her eyes and tried to forget. She could feel the pain creep up the back of her throat and she swallowed hard to try to contain it, but it was foul and deep. The visions were floating around in her brain, like a bad movie set on repeat. The tears were unstoppable. Waves of torment started to wrack her body as she gasped, the fear and realization of what she had just experienced surfacing. Her sobs caught her breath, and she cried—an ugly cry, one she could not control.

She heard knocking at her door, but she could barely walk. Nicholas had let himself in and by the look on his face, she knew he understood. He managed to reach her and caught her body as she collapsed into his arms, shattered and weak. She clung to him and cried, unable to move. He picked her up and carried her to the bed.

She wrapped her arms around him and buried her face into his chest, grateful for his warmth and losing herself in the safety of his strength. Nicholas laid her down on her pillow and Lucy could feel his strong hands cradle her face as he wiped away her tear-drenched cheeks.

"This is all my fault. I'm so sorry, Lucy. I know this is hard." Nicholas reached for her hand and held it tightly. He rubbed her arms as he begged her, "Please Lucy, take a deep breath. Breathe, honey, breathe."

Lucy could hear his words and feel his touch, but she was unable to look at him, her courage gone. Nicholas moved from the bed to the bathroom. She could hear the sink run and then shortly after, she felt a cold, damp cloth pressed against her face. She calmed herself, feeling the touch of Nick's hands on her body. She found peace in his attention, relaxing at his calming words and affection. She turned toward him, opening her eyes.

"Nick," she whispered, "Anthony and Rose." She could feel his worry as she took a deep, cleansing breath, catching the last hurtful sob in the center of her chest as she let out a pained sigh.

"I tried to save him, Lucy, but it was too late. If only he had listened to me. I tried, Lucy. I tried, but he's a fool. He never listens." Nicholas lowered his eyes as he continued to caress her cheek. Lucy focused on him. His pain was obvious; he had loved Anthony too.

"I wasn't expecting to feel so badly, Nick. I wasn't expecting this…to see all that. I mean, I knew it was possible, but you're never prepared…I wasn't prepared." She sobbed. "It was horrifying, Nick. I can't wrap my head around it."

Lucy lay back on her pillows, exhausted by the experience, her sobs quiet and her ability to speak being restored. Her eyes were tired and she wanted to feel loved. She wanted to feel like she was safe from her thoughts; she wanted to eradicate the visions of the night. She wanted to feel Nick's arms wrapped around her.

She wanted him, and she wanted him to make it all better for her.

"What about Rose, Nick? How will she manage without him? What about Jase, his son?" Lucy could feel the pain begin to surface again. Her tears seeped down the sides of her face as she looked into Nick's tortured eyes. He remained quiet; she knew he felt helpless, unable to fix what had just happened. He continued to stroke her face, wiping at her tears with one hand, holding Lucy's hand with the other.

"I'm sorry, Lucy. I'm so sorry." He leaned over her and kissed her cheeks. "I just want you to be okay. I can't believe I did this to you," he said. Lucy closed her eyes and felt his energy hovering over her. She wanted more; she needed him desperately. She wrapped her arms around his neck and pulled him closer.

She stared at him. "Please Nick, make the pain stop. Make it stop...I need you, Nicholas, please."

Nicholas responded instantly, covering her lips with his. He pressed his body on top of hers. She placed her hand on his face, and rubbing her thumb across his lower lip, she murmured, "Nick, I've thought about this so many times."

Lucy closed her eyes again and raised her arms up over her head as Nicholas peeled her shirt from her body. He pulled off his own shirt and unbuckled his pants, kicking off his heavy work boots and tossing them over to the side. Lucy slid her jeans off, flipping them across the room and then settled in next to Nicholas' comforting scent. She thought her heart would explode; her overactive imagination could never have prepared her for right now—the passion and intensity she felt for him, all the years she had thought about him.

She felt comfortable with him; she felt safe. His body was warm and strong as Lucy caressed his chest. She ran her hands up over his shoulders and down along his powerful arms, squeezing them gently. As he hovered over her, she could see the deep lines of age etched near his eyes and along his forehead.

"You've always been in my thoughts, Lucy. I may never get over you."

Lucy smiled, grateful for him and thankful for his distraction.

Nicholas kissed Lucy's neck, working his way down along her chest. He caressed her breasts with tiny kisses, massaging the skin. Placing his mouth over her nipple, he pulled on her. Lucy let out a small moan as he continued to tease her; she wrapped her legs around his body, feeling him intimately slip between them. She could feel the heat of his skin all over her. She wanted to take her time; she wanted this to last forever, to remember everything about him.

"Nick," she whispered, "I never want to forget this." Lucy opened her eyes again and met his stare. As he entered her body, she could feel him fill her insides, her belly flip-flopping with anxious anticipation.

"Oh my god, Nicholas."

He covered her lips again with his. She felt his tongue enter her mouth as he kissed her. Pausing, he rested his forehead on hers.

He continued to enter her as deep as he could go; slowly, he caressed her; slowly, he drove her insane. Her body begging for a release, she pleaded, "Oh god, Nick, please don't stop."

Nicholas grasped both her hands, moving relentlessly inside her, holding them over her head on the pillow. He kissed her lips one last time and then he took her over and over again. He entered her body with intensity, his eyes begging for mercy, begging for the pleasure to overtake him.

Lucy cried out, her emotions overcome by his need for her. She gave in to his passion and felt her body shatter in a relentless quake that rendered her helpless. The waves moved from her soul to his and she felt him shake above her. He moaned deeply, his powerful tone filling her with a deep satisfaction. They were lovers.

Nicholas collapsed on top of her, his breath still heavy, his chest now sweaty with healthy abandonment. Lucy wrapped herself even more deeply than before in his strong arms. She sunk into his chest as far as she could, seeking to feel the warmth of his body as it covered her like a blanket. They lay quietly listening to each other breathe, holding each other's hands. Time seemed to stand still for them, each aware that this moment would never happen again.

They waited for as long as they could before they reentered reality.

Nicholas lifted his head and searched for her lips. He kissed her, and whispered into her ear, "We need to go."

Lucy closed her eyes and felt the desperation of their situation come back to her. The pain she had experienced just ten minutes before resurfaced, and she knew that he was right. They were still in danger and they needed to go.

Lucy released her arms, which had been wrapped around Nick, but then paused, not wanting him to get up so quickly. She kissed him on his lips and said, "I love you, Nicholas."

He smiled deeply at her, grateful for her words. "I love you too, Lucy."

They both dressed and hurriedly left the hotel room, both of them deeply changed forever.

# CHAPTER 42

*Lucy*

It was a long flight from Mexico to Indiana with Nicholas by her side. He refused to let her return home without escorting her. He was concerned for her safety, but he was also uneasy about Jack and his reaction to her when she returned. Nick argued that he could help smooth things over and explain to Jack his motives for asking Lucy to come work for him. Lucy wasn't sure if that was going to be helpful, but she was just grateful that he sat next to her, that she could still see his face and feel his arm as it brushed up against hers.

There were so many things that she wanted to say to him, but words escaped her. Their eyes met often and she could feel the tension between them. He leaned into her repeatedly and asked her gently, "Are you okay?" His concern was touching, but Lucy's heart was breaking. This was going to be difficult—to return back home to her husband and family and to never, possibly ever see Nicholas again. She was not okay, but she had no choice.

Lucy tried her best to smile, a half attempt at hiding her feelings, and she knew that Nicholas understood this by the look of sadness evident in his own eyes. He reached for her hand and held it in his lap, wrapping his fingers around hers; he leaned back in his chair and closed his eyes. The trip seemed like a holiday dream turned into a nightmare, then turned back into the sweetest, most romantic vacation she had ever taken. The beautiful mountains that provided a backdrop to Chapala and its cobblestone roads, the shops and beautiful people...she would never forget it all. Her feelings were completely torn and jumbled, and wildly out of whack. The crushing reality of how empty her life would feel with Nicholas gone was something that only time would heal. She prayed for those moments to pass, that she might go back to that point in her life when she felt happy, when she loved Jack and her heart didn't ache so much.

She would never forget Nicholas; he made her feel strong again. He completed her in ways Jack was incapable of, he filled her spirit with the excitement of adventure, he inspired her to live and in many ways, he saved her. He was her catalyst and she loved him for that.

Their plane landed and, while Lucy waited outside the airport for Nicholas to pick her up in a car rental, she called home. The phone rang unanswered. Perhaps her family was out, maybe at Pop's? Guilty feelings and concern began to bombard her thoughts.

She considered being honest with Jack, telling him how she felt about him, about their marriage. Maybe it would bring them closer if they could have a real, honest conversation…to clear the air.

Lucy took a deep breath. Nick pulled up to the curb and she sat in the rental car. They drove through Indiana quietly, heading toward the farm. "Are you looking forward to seeing your children?" Nick asked with a smile.

"Are you kidding? I can't *wait* to hold my babies again. It's only been a few days, but it feels like I've been gone forever." Lucy paused. "What about you, Nick? Are things going to work out between you and Beth?"

Lucy watched his face. He shrugged his shoulders and a gloss of uncertainty covered his eyes. "She moved out, and I'm not sure if she'll come back. It's probably for the best." His sadness was thick, and her heart broke for him. She wished she could take care of him and support him the way he needed.

"I'm sorry, Nicholas. She doesn't know what she has." Lucy reached for his hand and held it in her lap.

It was dark when they arrived at her house on the hill. She took a deep breath and opened the door to the vehicle. The lights were dim; she wondered if anyone was home. She looked at Nicholas and they approached the porch. She knocked; no answer, so she opened the door.

"Hello! Is anyone here?" she called out. She glanced around the room and turned back to look at Nick. "They are probably at Pop's farmhouse, down the hill a ways. Do you mind, Nick?"

"No, of course not," Nick replied as he followed her back toward the car.

"I'm sorry; I just assumed that they would all be here. It's kind of late...I'm not sure why Jack would have the children out at this hour." Lucy thought for a moment. "Nick, before we go, I wanted to say goodbye, in case we don't get a chance to...ya know, after."

Nicholas put the keys into the vehicle and started the car. He glanced over at Lucy and smiled at her. "I don't want to say goodbye, Lucy. I don't want this to end. Perhaps we can stay in touch somehow. Maybe I can see you again."

Lucy leaned in, placed her hand on his cheek and kissed him. She lingered on his lips. "I would like that, Nick." Lucy appreciated his gentle way to say goodbye. Anything else would be far too difficult and she didn't want to feel desperate. They needed each other. Perhaps they could remain friends.

Nicholas drove down the hill past the cornfield and up the stone driveway into Pop's barnyard. They both got out of the car again, feeling the breeze at their backs as they walked toward the house.

Something was off.

The still of the night was concerning, and Lucy felt panic in her stomach. Her anxiety was always an indicator of danger. She stopped walking and looked at Nick.

"Something's not right, Nick. I have this weird feeling."

As soon as Lucy said the words, Charles came bounding out of Pop's farmhouse, gun in hand, grinning at the two of them.

"Well, well, well. Look who decided to show up after all?"

Charles pointed his gun at Lucy as he approached her.

"Charles!" she cried.

He swaggered along the path. It was obvious that he had been drinking.

She felt Nicholas bristle behind her. He was tense, perhaps looking for an opportunity to reach for his sidearm.

Her surprise turned into a concerned frown. "Where's Jack?" she asked aggressively, her eyebrows lowered. She didn't like the look on Charles' face and she had a gun pointed at her.

She looked around for her children, her eyes scanning the windows and the kitchen screen door, hoping to see one of their heads, but saw nothing. Her stomach sank and her heart was racing.

"Look who it is, honey!" Charles turned his head back toward the house and screamed for Kat to come out and join him. Kat opened the screen door and stepped out onto the front porch, her eye blackened and her clothing torn. Her face was somber; it was all Lucy could do not to run to her.

"Kat! Are you okay?" Lucy took a few steps forward but Charles stopped her in her tracks. He pointed his weapon at Lucy's chest and sauntered a bit closer to her. He then turned his gun toward Nicholas.

"Don't even think about it, Detective! I'm quite surprised that you would make an appearance here, after you persuaded my brother's wife to come work with you and God knows what else!" He grinned. "Jack's not too pleased with you, Lucy, although he's a little tied up right now, but I'm sure he wouldn't be too pleased." Charles waved his gun at Lucy, eyeing her up and down with a distasteful look.

Lucy knew he was trouble. It was a huge mistake, to ignore her instincts.

"Charles, please," she implored. "Put the gun down. Let's talk about this. I'm sure whatever is going on with you...we could all work it out. We are family here; we should support each other."

Charles laughed. He looked down at the ground and started to speak, seemingly to himself. He shook his head back and forth, he looked at Lucy and he kept repeating, "You don't know, you just don't know."

"I don't know what, Charles?" Lucy asked, her patience dissipating. "What is it?" Lucy looked up at Kat, who was crying. She was shaking her head no, as if the words Charles was about to say were unbelievable.

Charles started again, barely audible. His tone was soft and his voice staggered from the effects of alcohol. "Do you remember, Lucy, while we were in Boston looking for Kat, you and Nick, racing from state to state trying to save the day while I sat rotting in jail, waiting for the truth to come out?"

Charles looked up at Lucy. She could feel that he suffered; his pain festered in him like a boiling teakettle.

"I remember thinking, as I sat in that holding cell, that this was where I belonged. I felt comfortable there. I knew that you and Nicholas thought I was untrustworthy. I knew deep down inside you…that you feared I killed your sister. I understood then that you would never let go of that fear." He scoffed. "I figured you would hold it deeply and would always question my motives as a person."

Lucy shook her head. "Charles, I never thought that. I never thought you killed Kat. I don't know why you feel that way."

"It's not the point, Lucy. The truth is, you were right to think that I was untrustworthy. You were always right." He chuckled. "I am less of a person than you, and there's nothing that I say now that can fix this or correct what's been done. I killed Pop."

Lucy stared, her breath caught in her throat. The admission was shocking. But was it true?

"I killed him," he went on. "There's no fixing that, Lucy. No matter how hard we try, he's not coming back."

Charles staggered forward, looking at Lucy as if seeing the pain move across her face made everything he did worth it to him. Lucy looked over at Nick for confirmation, his face somber, his eyes wild with anger. She looked back at Charles, her mind racing. She wasn't sure that she believed him, but then she looked at Kat. Kat's shoulders shook uncontrollably; tears of pain ran down her face. Her sister nodded and Lucy knew then that it was true: Charles killed Pop. Lucy shook her head, opened her mouth slightly, trying to speak, but her words were silenced by the shock that ran through her body.

Nicholas took several steps closer to Lucy, and took out his gun, holding it on Charles the entire time. Charles continued to move carelessly, swinging his weapon between Lucy and Nick.

Charles eyed Nick's weapon and glared at his face. "Why don't you put the gun down, Nick. Kick it over here, toward me."

"I don't think so, Charles." Nick's tone was solid and certain.

"You think you're so smart." He chuckled. "You think you're such a great detective that you solve cases and put all the bad folk back in prison." Charles reached into his pocket, pulled out a cigarette, and lit it. His eyes locked with Nicholas and Lucy felt the anger ripple between them.

"I do my job, Charles," Nick countered. "I try my best to solve cases and put the right people behind bars. I've always been sorry for the mistakes we made with you, but they weren't big enough mistakes to warrant this behavior. I still don't understand why you would hurt your family like this."

Charles took a long drag and looked at the cigarette as he held it in between his thumb and his middle finger. He purposefully exhaled the cigarette smoke and started to snicker. "Tell me Nick, how does it feel?"

Nick looked on at Charles. "How does what feel?"

Charles stared at Nick long and hard and asked the question again. "How does it feel, Nick?"

Lucy could feel her heart race significantly. She thought back to that day—the look of pain he had in his eyes, when Nicholas explained to her how his house was destroyed and that someone had scrolled across his daughter's wall, *How does it feel, Nick?*

Registration of what Charles was insinuating started to settle over Nick's tortured face.

"Mr. Know It All Detective! Tell me, have you found the criminals who broke into your home, ruined your furnishings, and stole all of your electronics? You're a smart man. Have you solved *that* case yet? Your poor wife and children…they must have been devastated."

Nicholas stood his ground, his knuckles white, his finger on the trigger.

"You broke into my home? Why would you break into my home and destroy my things?"

"I needed you to fund a few things for me. I figured that it was a win-win situation: I could get a little revenge, which is what you deserved, and I needed money. It's not rocket science."

Charles waved his gun carelessly, swaying from side to side, barely standing straight. Lucy thought she could probably push him over. She watched him, looking for an opening.

"So, you broke into my home, Charles? It was you?"

"Yes, of course it was me. Who else would do such a thing?" Charles started to laugh at Nicholas' confused questions. He laughed so hard that he could barely breathe, propelling his cigarette-filled lungs into a smoker's coughing fit.

Lucy's eyes started to water. She thought about Rose, and the loss she suffered at the hands of her and Nick. It was their fault that Anthony was dead, nothing more than a great big mistake and misunderstanding. Charles had been the one at fault, all along.

She thought about Pop, and the suffering his death had caused her family. The loss overwhelmed her.

She ran toward Charles to attack him, punching at his chest and swinging at his face.

"You SON OF A BITCH! How could you? How could you?"

Charles grabbed Lucy by the hair and held her against his side as he pointed the gun at her head. He stared at Nick.

"Don't even think about it, Nick. I'll kill her, I swear."

She had made a critical mistake, she realized, but it was too late. She couldn't stop herself. Charles roped his arm around her neck and held her in a chokehold while Lucy grasped at his hands to try to get him to release her. He was relentless.

"Charles, let her go. It's me you want anyway," Nick volunteered. "Let her go and you and I could leave here together. I'll take you to the airport and get you on a plane out of here to anywhere you want. Just please, Charles...let her go."

Charles snickered at him while he whispered in Lucy's ear, "He thinks he can control this situation." He raised his head and yelled, "Forget it, Nick, I'm not leaving anywhere. This is my farm now. You hear me? This is my farm."

Lucy closed her eyes and prayed. She prayed hard for the strength to fight Charles.

Opening her eyes, she saw Susie Mae standing behind the big oak tree, which stood tall and strong, shadowing over the right side of the farmhouse. Over Susie's head was the bald eagle, perched in a frightening way, staring back down at her firmly. Susie Mae had a shotgun in her hand pointed straight for Lucy and Charles. Lucy acknowledged her and watched as Susie Mae lifted her chin toward the eagle.

The bird took flight and soared, flapping its wide, sturdy wings straight for Charles' body. The eagle propelled itself onto Charles, grasping its razor-sharp talons into Charles' shoulders, clawing into his back and ripping through his skin viciously.

Lucy ducked away from the flapping wings, tore herself out of Charles' grasp, and ran. She fell to the ground, crawling away in the dirt, taking refuge from her brother-in-law until Susie Mae and Nicholas shot.

The sound of guns exploding echoed over the hills.

Lucy watched Charles' body fall to the ground.

He landed solidly; he was down in moments.

The eagle hovered over him then soared up past Nicholas, circling around the barnyard before disappearing out of sight and beyond the orchards.

Lucy ran to Susie Mae and grabbed on to her. Nick was also at her side, both concerned with her well being and overly excited that she had appeared out of nowhere and helped put an end to the standoff.

Kat ran to Charles and knelt down besides him. With shaking hands, she reached down to check his pulse on the side of his neck.

"He's gone. He's not breathing." Kat slumped to the ground. She placed her hands over her face and started to cry.

Susie Mae pulled Lucy off of her and looked at her. "You okay, baby?"

"I'm fine." Lucy wiped away the tears in her eyes and tried to calm herself. It all happened so fast.

"Where are the children, where's Jack?" Susie Mae asked.

Lucy's eyes widened. "You don't know? Kat, where are my children?"

Kat remained unmoved and voiceless. Lucy shook her arm and pulled her to her feet. "Kat! Please, where are the kids?"

"They're in the house, Lucy," Kat sighed. "Charles would never do anything to hurt the kids. He loved the kids," she said, gulping. She shook her head. "I don't know where Jack is."

Lucy looked over at Nicholas, her worried eyes matching his.

"Go see to your children, Lucy," Nick instructed. "I'm going to scan the property for Jack. His truck is here. He must be somewhere. I'll find him."

"I'll go with you," Susie Mae stated. "We'll start in the barn."

Lucy ran up the front stairs of the porch and rushed into the kitchen, screaming for Anna. She could not find them on the first floor. She bounded up the stairs to the second floor and opened the first bedroom door. There they lay together, Sammy wrapped up in little Anna's arms, both asleep on the bed. Lucy collapsed on the side of the mattress and placed her hands on their tiny cheeks. She thanked the Lord for keeping them safe and for protecting them. She kissed them so not to disturb them and then returned downstairs to help Susie Mae and Nick look for Jack.

She could feel his energy; Jack was still alive. She ran out of the house to catch up with Nick when she saw them helping Jack walk out of the barn, his head bloodied and his body weak. She ran for him.

"Jack!"

As she approached him, he fell to the ground. She dropped next to him and held him in her arms.

"Jack, are you okay? He needs water, Susie," Lucy said. "Run and grab him some water and a wet towel."

Susie Mae hurried to the farmhouse to retrieve those items as Nick stood aside and watched Lucy tend to her husband.

"Jack, Jack, are you okay?" she asked as he lay back in pain.

He reached up to her and touched her face. "I didn't think you were coming back," he whispered.

"I'm here now, Jack. I'm here, I'm not going anywhere." Lucy could hear police sirens in the distance as she touched Jack's head, trying to inspect his injury. She could feel Nick standing behind her, watching her. His concern for Jack was genuine, and after he had determined that he would survive, he advised Lucy that he would go and check on Kat and the children.

Lucy was grateful for his help. She watched him as he walked away from her.

She turned back to Jack and held his hand.

"I'm sorry Jack," she whispered. "I'm so sorry."

"I love you."

"I love you too, Jack," she cried as she kissed his face.

# CHAPTER 43

*Lucy*

Months past slowly and Lucy and Jack settled back into their old life. She hadn't heard from Nicholas. She figured that if she hadn't heard from him, she should accept that—it was probably for the best. She often wondered if she was doing the right things. She wished the signs were more clear, that she had an obvious path toward the decisions that she needed to make, but the signs were blurry and confusing.

She sighed as she continued to make her bed. Nicholas consumed her thoughts; she'd lost hours of sleep, trying to decipher what she felt and if she should contact him. It was a daily struggle for her.

She had always been a romantic. Her time with Nicholas was a blessing, something that she would never forget, something that she would relive in her mind for the rest of her life. What he did for her was unexpected; he fulfilled her with a hope and a passion that had awakened her spirit. Her life was better for it; she felt whole again and courageous. She knew that she could stand on her own if she needed to.

Both she and Nicholas were married; he was a city boy, a Boston detective who lived an entirely different life than she. Lucy was a farm girl. She lived a simple life; she took care of her family, worked in her gardens, and cared for her home. She knew she had no drive to be a city girl, no desire to live the fast pace that Nicholas endured daily. But, she thought about him nonetheless. There was a vulnerability that they both shared; she was unafraid to speak her mind to him, to express herself regardless of the risk, and his energy captivated her.

It was complicated. He was careful.

She wished she had more time with Nick to get to know him and to figure it out, for the man he was today. But that was impossible. She accepted that her relationship with him was over, but it hurt just the same. Jack was the father of her children; he was her safety net, and he loved her. She was not regretful of her decision, but it didn't mean that she didn't love Nick. She did. She loved him deeply.

Lucy walked outside of her home and down her driveway toward the mailbox. Her sister had left to go back east to be with their father, who had grown elderly in his years. Kat had always been a wanderer; she had some healing to do over Charles, and Lucy worried for her. She wished that things had ended differently, that Kat had found the right man and that she could get married and have a family someday. She hoped to hear from her sister that their father was okay and that Kat was moving on.

The warm sun shined on Lucy's face. It had been a quiet afternoon and she was looking forward to sitting on her porch and watching the sunset with her children.

She opened the mailbox and there was a letter marked *LUCY NIMCHAK.*

She opened it. It was from Nicholas.

*Dear Lucy,*

*I received this in the mail a few days ago. I thought about you and I knew that I needed to send this to you. I was as surprised to receive it as you are now. I hope it brings you relief as it did me, to know that Anthony is alive and well.*

Lucy picked up a picture of Anthony and Rose. The picture was taken at a birthday party for Anthony, based on the birthday decorations and the cake in front of him. Rose leaned in next to him and smiled.

Lucy jumped as she looked at the photo. She could feel their happiness. She could feel Rose's beautiful spirit and the settled environment that her and Anthony shared. She closed her eyes and thanked god that he was alive. It was a true miracle that Anthony survived. Nicholas couldn't have given her a greater gift.

*I know you're happy right now, looking at this picture. Anthony turned thirty just last month. He is alive and well and looks healthy and happy.*

*I wanted you to know.*

*I hope that you are well too. I think of you often and I haven't forgotten our promise. I continue to look forward to the day we see each other again, and until then, you will always be on my mind.*

*Love always,*

*Nicholas*

Lucy held the letter tight to her chest. She read it again and followed the lines of Nicholas' handwriting with her finger, as if she could feel the pen that he held in his hand as it moved.

She loved him. She would never forget him.

The End

*Dear Reader,*

*With great gratitude, I wish to thank you for your time and for reading*
***Vintage Hearts.***

*I hope that you enjoyed it and I encourage you to follow me on*
*Facebook.com/SusanBRoara, Twitter, Instagram, Goodreads and Amazon's*
*author page Susan B. Roara.*

*I look forward to your reviews and comments.*

*Thank you!*

*Susan B. Roara*